STARTING OVER IN KEY WEST: SHADOWS OF YESTERDAY

A Key West Romance Novel – Book 2

AMY RAFFERTY

STAY UPDATED WITH ME

Thank you so much for purchasing or downloading my book! I am grateful to all my amazing readers.

To stay updated on all my latest books, newsletters, freebies and beautiful photos from the fabulous locations I write about, why not join my VIP group?

I will send you regular pictures of La Jolla Cove, San Diego and the Florida Gulf Beaches where I try to spend as much time as I can. I live in San Diego, my own 'Garden Of Eden' and I am in love with the sea and the beaches in the area. They inspire me to write lots of beachy mystery romance fiction to share with my awesome readers like you. To join me go to https://landing.mailerlite.com/webforms/landing/y6w2d2

You will be asked for your email. You also get a FREE BOOK whenever you sign-up!

CHARACTER LIST

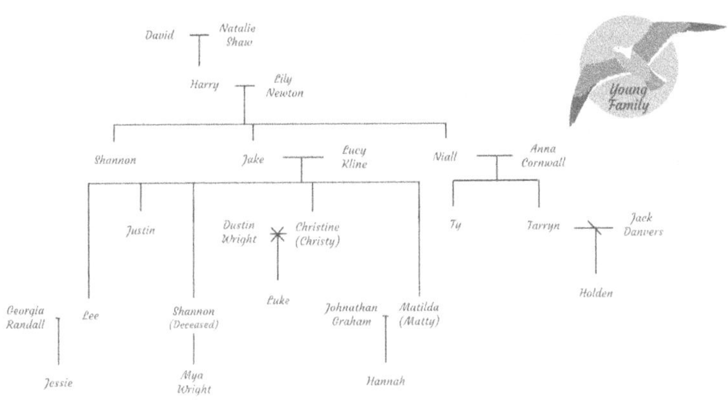

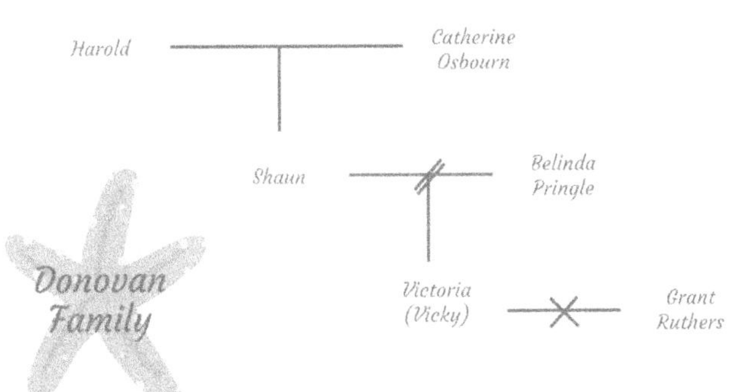

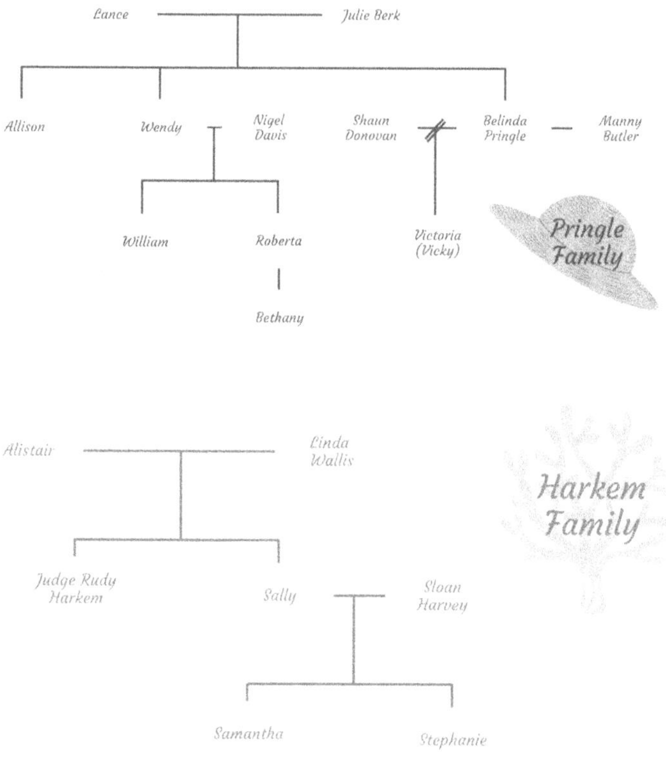

Dr. Tara Bright - Luke Young's Lady Love

Mrs. Amelia (Rodriguez) Parish - Owned the dance studio

Robin Kelly - Works for Vicky
Oliver Kelly - Robin's son/Jessie's boyfriend

Angela Keene - Lee Young's ex-girlfriend

Dante Alverez - Works for Vicky
Cory Alverez - Works for Vicky

Agent Garry - Vicky's trusted mysterious Agent

DA Joshua Armstrong - Retired

Ian Gilbert - Jessie's high school boyfriend

Chapter One

A SURPRISE VISITOR

*V*icky Ruthers walked up the familiar path to the front door of the rambling Victorian house where she'd spent her childhood visiting her best friend, Christy Young. Although Vicky had come back for Christy's father's funeral the previous year, she hadn't been able to stay for the reception. The last time Vicky had been in the Young's house was thirteen years ago, but again, that was not a happy occasion. Christy's mother Lucy Young had passed away after struggling with cancer.

Tonight, Vicky was here to surprise Christy. She did have a mission, but that wasn't for tonight; that was for tomorrow. Tonight, she was going to enjoy the company of her second family and unwind from the most grueling and emotionally challenging two years of her life. She repositioned the two bottles of champagne she had beneath her arm and pushed the doorbell.

After a few minutes of no one answering, Vicky looked at her watch. The Youngs would be having dinner around this time. Her stomach growled, reminding her she hadn't eaten the entire day as she had been on the go since she'd opened her eyes at three that morning. Vicky rang the bell again, and a few minutes later, the door swung open.

"Will you look at that, Aaron Butler in the flesh!" Vicky raised an eyebrow, looking up at Aaron.

"Hello, Vicky," Aaron greeted her, a frown creasing his handsome brow.

Aaron looked unsure of what he should do. Christy had already filled Vicky in on what was happening with her, her kids, and Aaron, so she knew Christy and Aaron were dating again. She saw Aaron hesitate for a few seconds and took pity on him by stepping up to him and giving him a hug.

"Welcome home, step-brother." Vicky laughed, stepping back and seeing the shocked expression on his face. "Are you going to stand there gaping at me or step aside and let me in? I'm starving, and I know the Youngs have dinner at this time."

Aaron stepped aside and let Vicky in. Vicky walked past Aaron and followed the noise into the dining room. She could hear Aaron following behind, but he was forgotten the moment Vicky stuck her head through the dining room door, and Mya spotted her.

"Aunt Vicky!" Mya Young, Christy's daughter and eldest child, squealed, jumped up, and ran to hug Vicky.

"Vicky!" Christy Young spun around, sprung up, and rushed over to Vicky. "I wasn't expecting you until the week before Christmas." She hugged Vicky. "What a lovely surprise."

After a round of greetings, hugs, and introductions to some of the people around the table she didn't know, a place was set for Vicky at the table. Vicky was wedged between Christy and Malcolm Bright, a lieutenant at Christy's fire station, where Christy was the acting battalion chief. As always, there was plenty of food, and Vicky helped herself to the wonderful spread while Christy caught her up on the latest news.

"How long are you home for, Vicky?" Lee Young, Christy's older brother, asked her from across the table.

Vicky looked over at Lee, but before she could answer, Lee's girlfriend, Samantha Harvey, butted in, "Lee, darling, why don't you let the poor woman eat. Clearly, she's starving as she's on her second helping of mashed potatoes." Samantha's cold green eyes narrowed on Vicky.

"You try them," Vicky smiled sweetly at the vapid blonde

clinging to Lee's side like a vine in need of support. "The Youngs make the best potatoes in Key West." She put a spoonful in her mouth and made a show of tasting them. "At a guess, I'd say Pops made these."

"You're spot on there, Vicky, my dear," Pops, Christy's grandfather, beamed at her when he heard his name being mentioned. "But Samantha watches her carb intake." He raised his eyebrows at Samantha. "Unlike you, who has never had to diet in her life!"

"Oh, gosh no," Vicky said in disgust. "I love my food far too much."

"Vicky's always had a metabolism like a teenager." Lee laughed, trying to defuse a potentially nasty situation. Vicky could see he was sensing Samantha's hackles rising. "To answer your question, Lee, I'm home for good. I've taken over the dance studio from Mrs. Amelia!"

"Oh, Vicky, that's amazing!" Christy hugged Vicky. "It's going to be so nice to have you back in the same town again after all these years."

"I know," Vicky said to Christy.

Vicky turned her attention away from Samantha Harvey, who Vicky was sure to cross paths with again in the near future. In fact, Vicky was counting on it. She'd been shocked, although not surprised, to see Samantha Harvey sitting at the Young's dinner table. Christy had told Vicky that Lee was seeing Samantha, but Christy had also told Vicky it wasn't serious and that Lee hadn't even introduced the woman to his daughter after nine months of dating. Christy hadn't mentioned anything more about Lee and Samantha, and Vicky didn't want to pry or seem like she was interested in knowing about them.

"So, you're still dancing?" Lee pulled Vicky's attention back to him, and once again, Vicky's eyes clashed with Samantha's venomous green ones.

"I never stopped dancing," Vicky told Lee, giving him a beautiful smile, knowing she was teasing the viper clinging to him. *That's one way to get her attention*, Vicky thought to herself.

"Vicky has traveled all over America dancing the lead for

many big shows," Christy said proudly. "She only stopped four or five years ago for personal reasons."

"Yes, but I started a dance school at my Hibiscus Island home in Miami," Vicky deliberately name-dropped and smiled to herself when she saw Samantha was taking the bait. *Oh, this is going to be easier than I thought!*

"Oh, you owned a property on Hibiscus Island?" Samantha took a swallow of her wine.

"She did," Christy answered for Vicky. "She sold the property a few months ago, isn't that right, Vicky?" She turned and gave Vicky a look that said she knew what Vicky was doing and was wondering why.

"I did," Vicky confirmed Christy's statement. "Christy, do you think we should open the champagne?"

"Yes, that's a brilliant idea," Christy said through a false smile.

"I can do it," Aaron offered.

"Oh, no, you sit and relax," Christy smiled at Aaron and gave him a kiss. "Vicky and I will be right back."

"Don't eat all the roasted chicken," Vicky said to Lee. "Or at least not all the white meat."

"I'll try not to," Lee grinned and deliberately took a chicken breast.

"Do you think you should have any more meat?" Vicky and Christy heard Samantha say to Lee.

"Did you see Jessie's face when Samantha said that to Lee?" Vicky widened her eyes and shook her head. "Good grief, what is Lee doing with that viper?"

"Okay, spit it out... what is going on?" Christy crossed her arms and leaned back against the kitchen counter, looking at Vicky questioningly.

"I don't know what you're talking about!" Vicky said innocently.

"Come on, Vicky, I know you well enough to know when you're baiting someone into doing something that will either expose them or have them make a fool of themselves."

"I just don't like her and the way she talks for or over Lee." Vicky shrugged and started opening the champagne.

"Okay." Christy's eyes narrowed as she watched Vicky. "Have it your way, but I will figure out what you're up to." She raised her eyebrows. "You know there was a time we told each other everything. Well, right up until you went and studied criminology and...."

"I thought you two may need a hand," Jessie interrupted Christy. "Please say you need a helping hand!"

"Of course," Vicky turned and grinned at the beautiful young woman.

Jessie was the spitting image of her mother, Georgia Randall, Lee's wife, who disappeared twenty-two years ago when Jessie was two. Like Georgia, Jessie was five-foot-six, petite, with a mane of lush deep red hair and startling green eyes. Jessie was also super intelligent like her mother was. Georgia had been a rocket scientist, who after getting her degree, decided she wanted to be a cryptographer and, after graduating, had been snapped up by K W Research Facility.

Jessie was studying to become a geneticist. Vicky had recently learned that Jessie had accepted a job at the same lab Georgia had worked for when she'd disappeared. Vicky had been asked by some concerned entities to look into the reasons behind the job offer and make sure they were legitimate. After all these years, the circumstances around Georgia's disappearance were still suspicious.

"Vicky?" Christy touched Vicky's arm. "Are you okay? You went off into your own world there for a while."

"I'm fine," Vicky assured Christy. "I was just marveling at how much Jessie looks like Georgia."

"Thank you," Jessie gave a little curtsey. "I'll take that as a compliment as my mother was beautiful."

"Yes, she was!" Christy smiled at her niece.

"So why are you hiding out in the kitchen?" Vicky asked Jessie, popping open the bottle.

"It's a long story, Aunt Vicky," Jessie said with a shudder.

"Let me guess... you don't like your father's girlfriend?" Vicky guessed correctly.

"Don't get me wrong, I'm glad Dad is dating again, but that woman...." Jessie gave another shudder. "There is just something about her that doesn't seem right. Plus, she's all over Dad like a vine and hardly lets him talk to anyone when she's around."

"I noticed that and thought the same thing." Vicky shook her head and started to pour the champagne. "She's also very rude in that she has no problem just butting into a conversation."

"Exactly!" Jessie agreed. "I also feel like she hates how close my dad and I are. When he came to Boston to help me pack this last time, she was constantly on the phone with him."

"I believe she's a lawyer in the DA's office like your dad?" Vicky finished the first bottle of champagne and went to open the second one.

"Yes, and she's dead-set against my father taking over Uncle Shaun's law practice with Luke," Jessie told Vicky. "I think it will be awesome for my dad to take over Donovan Law."

"I couldn't agree more," Vicky said. "My father told me that Lee would give him an answer in a few weeks because Lee wanted to discuss it with you first."

"More like discussing it with Samantha!" Jessie said with a hint of bitterness. "Since she's come into his life, he's started to change."

"What do you mean?" Christy asked Jessie, her brows knitting together in a frown.

"It just seems that Dad is constantly walking around on eggshells," Jessie explained. "When he was in Boston, he missed a call from Samantha because we were at lunch, and she was not happy about it. I heard him tell her that he was with me, and she was shouting so loud I could hear her through the phone."

"Wow," Vicky took a sip from one of the glasses and handed another to Christy, then Jessie.

"She told him that I was an adult now, and he needed to put himself first for a change," Jessie took a sip of the bubbly liquid.

"I bet that didn't go down well with Lee?" Christy looked at her niece with a worried frown on her brow.

"My dad said nothing. He changed the subject and then excused himself from the table to finish the conversation." Jessie's eyes narrowed in anger as she took another sip of her drink.

"That's not like Lee at all." Christy's frown deepened. "How many times has he tried to date, and as soon as the woman said anything he thought was remotely against Jessie that he'd call it quits?"

"Yes, do you remember Angela?" Vicky's eyes widened. "We pushed your father to start dating again when you were thirteen."

"Angela?" Jessie's brow drew together as she thought back.

"Oh, yes. He liked Angela. She was so sweet, and she ran an art gallery in town," Christy reminded Jessie.

"Oh, yes!" Jessie remembered. "She was all sweet and nice around Dad or the rest of the family, but as soon as your backs were turned, she became a shrew. She loved to tell me how when she married Dad, she was going to send me to some remote boarding school."

"When you told your father what she was doing, she broke down into tears and told him you were a terror to her," Vicky said.

"That's when I bugged the house." Jessie laughed. "I caught her on the nanny cam doing her wicked witch routine to me."

"Your father was furious and told her in no uncertain terms that his daughter, no matter how old, would always come first in his life!" Christy shook her head. "Angela was not happy. She bombarded us all with messages for days after that, asking us to help her sort this mess out with Lee."

"As if we would do that!" Vicky huffed.

"Hi," Samantha's voice startled the three of them. "I just came to see what was taking so long. I need to go home soon. I have an early court appointment tomorrow."

"Oh, that's a shame," Jessie said with a sweet smile. "We were just bringing the champagne and ice cream out. We won't be long."

"Well, let me help!" Samantha stepped into the kitchen. "I love this old house." She looked at Christy. "Lee tells me the family lets you stay here with your kids?"

"Uh..." Christy looked at Samantha, a little taken aback by the question.

"Usually, the property would go to the oldest in the family, and that would be Lee, right?" Samantha glanced around the kitchen again. "There is so much you could do with this kitchen space, and the house is in a prime real estate area."

"Actually, the house belongs to *all* my grandchildren!" Pops' voice, although not raised, seemed to crack through the kitchen. "Nothing can be done to the house without the other's consent, and that trickles down to even the youngest of my great-grand-children."

"It's a lovely place to raise children," Samantha turned and smiled at Pops. She wasn't one bit fazed by his icy look. "You never know... you may have one more grandchild in the near future after Lee and I are married."

Samantha smiled smugly at Jessie, winked at Pops, patting his shoulder as she walked out of the kitchen.

"Did she just say what I think she said?" Jessie's cheeks were flaming red, and her green eyes blazed with anger. "Does she really think she can have children at her age?"

"Jessie, calm down, honey," Pops said soothingly and walked into the kitchen. "Samantha is just trying to stir you up."

"Did she say after she and Lee get married?" Vicky's eyes widened in shock. "Not if but after?"

"I'm sure she meant if they get married!" Christy said, trying to diffuse the situation.

"No, she meant when!" Jessie's eyes were narrowed danger-ously on the door. "She has no chance of marrying my dad, espe-cially if I have anything to do with it."

"Jessie!" Alarm bells went off in Vicky's mind when she saw the look on Jessie's face. "What are you planning?"

"I don't like how she's trying to change my father. It's like she has some hidden agenda," Jessie said, making the alarm bells in Vicky's head get even louder. "I'm going to find out what it is and expose the viper."

"I don't think that you should meddle, love," Christy warned Jessie. "I'm sure Lee is intelligent enough to figure out that Samantha is not a nice person all on his own."

"Of course, Aunt Christy, you're right!" Jessie gave Christy a smile. "My dad is a grown man, and I have to back off." She picked up a tray of champagne. "I'll take these through."

"Thank you, honey," Christy said, watching Jessie intently.

"I know my great-granddaughter...." Pops leaned down and picked up another tray of drinks. "And she didn't mean a word of what she just said. We're going to have to watch that girl. She's up to something!"

"I couldn't agree with you more, Pops!" Vicky sighed. This was a complication Vicky was not expecting.

Pops walked out of the kitchen with the last tray of champagne while Christy dished up the ice cream.

"Should I speak to Lee?" Christy finished scooping ice cream into the final bowl while Vicky put them onto a tray along with the berries and chocolate sauce.

"No," Vicky said emphatically. "Definitely not!"

"I'd hate to see Jessie getting hurt because of Samantha." Christy put the ice cream back into the freezer.

"I think we should do as Pops suggested and keep an eye on the situation," Vicky suggested. "We don't want to escalate anything by interfering."

"You're right!" Christy sighed and picked up one of the two trays of dessert. "I'm so glad you're home."

"Me too," Vicky said honestly. "I've needed this." She smiled, hearing the laughter coming from the dining room. "It was getting really lonely back in Miami without Grant."

"I know how that feels," Christy said compassionately. "I found my heart healed a lot quicker when I was surrounded by family."

"I think we should get this ice cream to the masses before we have a mutiny on our hands!" Vicky laughed and followed Christy through to the dining room.

The rest of the evening flew by with the Young family and their friends playing a friendly game of charades after dinner was over, and everyone helped clean up. Samantha had gone home by then, cleverly timing her departure to be before the cleanup. After she'd left, the tension in the house seemed to lessen by one hundred percent.

As they sat in the lounge playing the final round of charades, Vicky's eyes fell on Lee, who was sitting next to Jessie on the sofa. Since Samantha had left, Lee seemed a lot more relaxed, although he'd checked his phone every few minutes. Vicky really hoped what Samantha had hinted at about Lee and her getting married wasn't true. As Jessie suspected, there was most definitely something off about Samantha Harvey.

After the final round of the game, Vicky announced that it was time for her to go home. Christy and Aaron offered to walk her home.

"I'll say it again and again," Christy and Vicky were walking arm in arm with Aaron next to Christy. "I'm so glad you're home, Vicky. I've dreamed of us living up the street from each other again for years."

"It looks like that dream is going to come true," Vicky told Christy. "My father is moving to Key West Seaside Retirement Village, and I told him I'd take over the house."

They stopped at the Donovan house front gate.

"Vicky, that's amazing!" Christy smiled. "I know your dad has been saying how difficult it's getting to look after the old house on his own."

"He wants to retire and be surrounded by people his own age, not holed up in an old rambling house," Vicky explained.

"I can't think of your dad retired!" Aaron said. "I've never seen anyone as passionate about their job as your father."

"He has always been married to the law!" Vicky sighed. "I hope that Lee takes him up on his offer to take over Donovan

Law. I know my dad would love nothing more than to let Luke take over, but he's worried that Luke doesn't have the experience."

"I know," Christy nodded. "I think Lee really wants to leave the DAs office and was so excited when your father made the offer."

"I believe it's his new girlfriend that is holding him back from making that decision," Aaron confided in them. "Seems she has bigger plans for him like running for mayor and then on to bigger political things."

"Really?" Vicky looked up at Aaron in surprise. "That's interesting."

"And the first I'm hearing of this!" Christy looked up at Aaron accusingly. "Why didn't you tell me this?"

"Lee and I are just patching up our friendship," Aaron defended his actions. "I didn't want to blurt out everything we've been catching up about."

"I'm glad you're back in the family fold, Aaron," Vicky told him honestly. "For what it's worth, I'm glad I was wrong about you."

"Thanks!" Aaron looked at her with raised brows.

"I'm going to say goodnight. I've had a long day and need to get my beauty rest." Vicky stifled a yawn. "I have so much to start organizing."

"Well, come over for dinner tomorrow night and bring your father," Christy invited her.

"That would be great," Vicky leaned forward for a hug from Christy and Aaron. "Although I was going to come for dinner, anyway." She grinned.

"I know," Christy laughed. "It took my father a long time to stop glancing at the door, waiting for your dinner-time knock on the door after you left."

"My father was a horrible cook, so we'd invite ourselves to the Youngs table most nights," Vicky explained to Aaron. "But then you already know this because, if I'm not mistaken, you were there most nights too before yours and Lee's fall out."

"That's right." Aaron grinned. "The Youngs always had such a great atmosphere that it made my home life feel cold and empty."

"My dad filled our house with as much love as he could, but there were still so many empty spaces in the house," Vicky's eyes shadowed over. "But the Young house always seemed to be filled to the brim and was bursting with family and love."

"We were both very lucky to have grown up with the Young family," Aaron wrapped his arms around Christy and kissed the top of her head.

"We were lucky to have such good friends like the two of you," Christy told them.

"It's getting chilly." Vicky shuddered. "I best be getting in, and you two need to get inside. I'll see you tomorrow."

Vicky turned and walked into her house, turning to wave at Christy and Aaron, who'd waited to see her into her house safely.

Chapter Two

THE SECRET WOMAN IN THE BOARDROOM

"Vicky, is that you?" Shaun Donovan's voice came from the upstairs landing.

"Hi, Dad!" Vicky called up the stairs. "I'm sorry to wake you."

"No, I wasn't asleep," Shaun assured her. "Would you like a cup of cocoa?"

"I'd love that," Vicky smiled at her father as he walked down the stairs.

At seventy-four, Shaun Donovan was still a tall, handsome man married to his work and dedicated to his only daughter. He wasn't into bodybuilding or the gym, but he ran and did regular push-ups, sit-ups, and chin-ups each day. Even now, he still made sure he kept his heart going and body in the best shape he could.

Shaun's father had left them the Donovan house on Queen Street. Vicky's grandfather had also been a lawyer, but he was into corporate law and was a partner in a big law firm in Miami. Grandfather Donovan's wife preferred Key West, which was where she was born, so Vicky's grandfather would live between Miami and Key West. Shaun had admired how well his parents had made that situation work for them. But Shaun wanted to be closer to his family and had started Donovan Law.

Vicky's grandfather had joined her father in the firm ten

years before he retired and had built it into a reputable firm that both the rich and normal people could afford. Vicky smiled as she remembered the first time she'd told someone her father's law firm looked after both the rich and poor. Shaun had told her that he'd always found the word poor to be demeaning and preferred to say normal people. Soon Shaun and her grandfather had clients from all over the Florida Keys, and when Vicky's grandfather had retired, Christy's mother, Lucy, had joined Donovan Law.

Lucy had lived in the Wilks' house when she was growing up. Christy's maternal grandmother was the oldest of the Wilks' daughters and had inherited the house with her sister, who was the current owner. Lucy and Shaun had grown up together and were the best of friends. When they went off to college, Shaun met Belinda Pringle, a history major and Vicky's mother. Lucy had always had a crush on the rugged Jake Young, who lived across the road, but Shaun and Lucy were two years younger than Jake, so they never hung out in the same circles.

The same year that Shaun met Belinda, Lucy had gotten together with Jake Young. Lucy and Jake were married two years before Shaun and Belinda. But Vicky and Christy were born six months to the day apart. Vicky was born in June, and Christy and her twin sister Shannon were born in December. Shannon had passed away tragically thirty years ago after giving birth to Mya, who Christy and her husband Dustin had adopted as her own.

"Vicky, have you heard a word I've been saying?" Shaun put a cup of steaming hot cocoa in front of her.

"I'm sorry, Dad," Vicky put a dash of honey in the cocoa. "I was miles away. I have so much to do, and I'm exhausted."

"I know, honey," Shaun sat down at the table in front of her. "So, tell me how you're really doing?"

"I get better every day, Dad," Vicky assured her father. "I'm so glad I'm home."

"You have no idea how glad I am that you're here too," Shaun said, sipping his cocoa.

"Tomorrow I get the keys to the dance studio." Vicky idly stirred her drink. "As far as I can see, Mrs. Amelia kept the place in top order and repaired."

"Oh, yes," Shaun agreed with Vicky. "Amelia has always kept that place top-notch. She adored you, you know. She was so pleased when you made an offer on the studio, so she didn't have to list it or worry who it was going to be sold to."

"Mm," Vicky looked at her father over the rim of her cocoa. "Mrs. Amelia tells me that she's also moving into Key West Seaside Retirement Village."

"Yes," Shaun confirmed. "I believe she is."

"Dad!" Vicky put her coffee cup down and looked at her father in exasperation. "Isn't it time you and Mrs. Amelia just come clean about your relationship?" She smiled at the stunned look on her father's face and took a sip of her drink. "Dad, it's been, what? Thirty-six years?" She shook her head. "Don't you think it's time you at least invited her home to meet me as your girlfriend?"

"I..." Shaun's cheeks were red. "How long have you known?"

"Oh..." Vicky shrugged. "Since I was fourteen. You know, the year you and Mrs. Amelia started sneaking around!" She gave him a smug grin. "I think the entire town knows but has been respectfully keeping your secret."

"Why didn't you say anything?" Shaun's eyes were huge with worry as he looked at his daughter.

"Like the entire population of Key West that knows both of you, I was respecting your privacy." Vicky put her hand over his. "I was delighted when I found out you and Mrs. Amelia were seeing each other. I always hoped she'd become my new mom, but you seemed adamant to keep quiet about your relationship."

"Honey..." Shaun's cheeks went redder.

"Dad, I think it's time!" Vicky insisted. "I would love for you to have a Christmas engagement." She stopped talking and looked at him with wide eyes. "After Christy's surprise fiftieth, though. Now you will bring Mrs. Amelia as your plus one. Although she was invited anyway."

"We're too old for all that now," Shaun said, waving it off. "We're content with our relationship as it is. You know we were both married before. Your mo... Belinda left me when you were only eight, and Amelia's husband was killed in the army."

"What has that got to do with anything?" Vicky raised her eyebrows. "Those are just excuses that I think the both of you have been using in order to protect me." She smiled knowingly at Shaun as his cheeks reddened even more. "Dad, I'm a grown woman, and even back then, I would've loved to see you happy again."

"You were so cut up when your mo... Belinda left us," Shaun said softly. "I never wanted to see you get hurt like that ever again, even if it meant I kept my relationship with Amelia secret." He smiled at her. "Amelia agreed with me. Especially because after the day Belinda walked out the door, you never referred to her or let anyone refer to her as your mother."

"Dad, I loved Mrs. Amelia. Even back then, before the two of you were dating, it was Mrs. Amelia who helped me sort out my aggression, anger, and hurt over Belinda leaving us," Vicky told him. "Long before you and Mrs. Amelia started dating, she'd already become my surrogate mother. I used to dream that she was my mother."

"I think seeing how you were with Amelia and how patient, kind, and loving she was with you was one of the reasons I fell in love with her," Shaun admitted. "She went out of her way to help you get over Belinda's leaving. She once told me that you were the daughter she'd always wanted to have, and although she hadn't been blessed to have her own children, she'd been blessed to have you in her life."

"Mrs. Amelia reminded me of Christy's mother." Vicky gave a soft laugh. "Do you know that when Christy and I were ten, we would pretend that Mrs. Amelia was my mother? So, when we found out you and she were actually dating four years later...."

"Well, that makes sense now," Shaun's brows drew together. "When you and Christy were fourteen, you'd always invite Amelia to come to have ice cream with us." His eyes widened even more as it dawned on him. "That's why you two always insisted I pick you both up from dance recitals. Was Lucy in on this?"

"Yes!" Vicky sighed. "It was Aunt Lucy that made me and Christy promise to let you and Mrs. Amelia take your relationship at your own pace and never mention it until either of you did."

"Looks like you broke that promise, then!" Shaun gave her a sly grin.

"No," Vicky shook her head. "We did not."

"I beg to differ, young lady!" Shaun raised his eyebrows. "I never brought up my relationship with Amelia tonight. You did that," he pointed out and winked at her.

"Clever," Vicky noted. "But you sort of hinted at the relationship," she said smugly.

"Fine," Shaun relented. "I know that you're going to twist everything to point this back at me. That's why I always said you should've gone into law."

"I did study law, Dad," Vicky reminded him. "I also took criminology and worked with forensics for a while, but my passion has always been dance, and that's why I got more out of my fine arts degree."

Vicky hated lying to her father. Well, she wasn't really lying. She did own and run a dance studio in Miami. But that was only one of Vicky's careers, and the only other person that knew about the other part of her career was Christy, who'd found out quite by chance.

"Do you really think I'm not too old to be getting married again after all these years?" Shaun changed the subject.

"Not at all. You're never too old to tie the knot or start a new chapter in your life, no matter how long or short that chapter may be," Vicky assured him. "Look at Pops. Did you know he's been dating Manny Butler's older sister Alma?"

"I did, actually," Shaun admitted. "I'm so happy for them both. Especially Alma. She may have been twenty years older than Manny, but he ruled her entire life."

"I'm happy for them too," Vicky agreed. "Pops seems in top spirits these days, and he's in his nineties."

"I guess you're right," Shaun said with a smile. "I'm so glad you know about Amelia. How about I invite Amelia over for dinner tomorrow night? We can get take out as none of us are good cooks."

"I've got a better idea!" Vicky grinned at her father. "We've been invited to the Young's for dinner. As they are our extended family, they'll be delighted to know you are happy and finally going legit with your relationship."

"I'll run it past, Amelia," Shaun promised. "Now, I think you should get to bed."

"I agree!" Vicky stood up with her cup of cocoa. "We both should as we both have big, grueling days tomorrow!"

Vicky waited for her father, who was about to follow her up the stairs but stopped and looked at her suspiciously with his brows furrowed. "What do you mean about me having a grueling day?"

Vicky hadn't realized what she'd said, and she'd let her guard down, having been so relaxed talking to her dad. "That you always have a grueling day at work because you're a lawyer!" She managed to cover up her slip of the tongue.

"Of course!" Shaun closed his eyes for a second and shook his head. Vicky could see he'd been genuinely shocked and worried that she knew something.

"Is something wrong, Dad?" Vicky looked at him curiously.

"No, I'm sorry, honey," Shaun said with a sigh. "I've got this really important case that has to be kept under the radar, and there are a lot of things that could go wrong, so I'm just being paranoid."

"It's okay, Dad, I understand." Vicky walked up to him and kissed him on the cheek. "Although, now you've got me really intrigued about the case." She gave him a cheeky grin and started walking up the stairs.

"You know I can't discuss it with you." Shaun followed Vicky up the stairs. "I just hope that it's over as quickly as can be," he breathed out, "for everyone's sake," he muttered, thinking Vicky couldn't hear him.

$\mathcal{L}$ee walked into Donovan Law. He had a ten o'clock appointment with Shaun Donovan. As Lee walked through the office, he looked around. He'd always liked this office. Lee used to come here with his mother when he was a young boy. He used to love listening to his mother and Uncle Shaun's legal jargon. They were the reason Lee became a lawyer. He wanted to be in family law just like them, but the best-laid plans and all that....

Lee sighed as he walked up to June, Shaun's office manager. "Good morning, Mr. Young," June greeted Lee with a warm smile. "You're right on time as usual."

"Hello, June," Lee greeted her. "You're looking lovely as always."

"Thank you, Mr. Charmer." June blushed. "Follow me, and I'll take you through to his office. He'll be with you in a few minutes. Shaun and your nephew are with a client in the main boardroom at the moment."

They walked past the large boardroom that June had said Luke and Shaun were in with a client. The blinds were drawn on the glass and the few glass panels of the room. But there was one section where the blinds were not completely closed, and Lee could see into the room. He couldn't resist taking a quick look and froze when he saw the woman with her back to him. Long, deep rich red hair hung down around her shoulders and reminded him so much of.... He stopped himself and pulled away as June turned to see where he was.

"You know you shouldn't be peaking in on a meeting with our clients!" June admonished him. "Now, come on, before you get me into trouble."

"Who is the client?" Lee knew it was unethical, but he

couldn't stop himself from asking. "She has the exact same color hair as Ge...." Lee swallowed. "Jessie."

"I don't know who she is," June admitted. "The staff had to wait in the break room while a U.S. Marshal escorted the lady into the offices. We were told she's under protective custody, and it's best for all of us if we don't know who she is."

June pushed Shaun's office door open and led Lee inside.

"Was it Justin who brought her in?" Lee asked June. "I know he's in town."

"No, it was a female Marshal. She's in there with them at the moment." June turned to leave the office. "Would you like a cup of coffee?"

"Do you still roast your own coffee beans?" Lee asked June.

"Of course." June looked offended that he'd even have to ask her that. "You ask me that every time you come here."

"I just want to make sure it's your special roast." Lee grinned at her. "As it is your special roast, I would love a cup, please, June." Lee watched June leave Shaun's office door open when she left.

Lee craned his neck to try and see into the conference room, but other than that small part of the blinds that were open in the conference room, he couldn't see much. Lee's mind raced, wondering who the woman sitting in the conference room was. Jessie and her mother both had thick, silky, deep rich red hair, just like the woman in that room.

Lee was sure there were millions of women in the world with the same color hair, but there was something familiar about the woman in the conference room. In the brief glimpse Lee had gotten of her, she'd flicked her hair in the same way that.... Lee closed his eyes and clenched his jaw. It had been twenty-two years since Lee's wife, Georgia, had disappeared.

Jessie had been two when Georgia had vanished into thin air. Lee still remembered that day like it was yesterday. Nothing had seemed out of the ordinary. Lee and Georgia's marriage was still strong, and they were still very much in love. Georgia had been Lee's high school sweetheart. Georgia, Lee, and Jessie had eaten breakfast together, and she'd kissed him goodbye and dropped Jessie off at preschool like Georgia always did. She had let him know that Jessie had happily gone to school and that she was on her way to work.

Lee had had quite a grueling court schedule that day and hadn't noticed the time until Jessie's school had phoned him. It was four o'clock in the afternoon, and Georgia was two hours late picking up Jessie, and the school had had no luck getting ahold of her. That's when Lee noticed that he hadn't heard from Georgia the entire day either. Lee had dropped everything and gone to get his baby girl.

Lee had also tried numerous times to get ahold of Georgia on the way to get Jessie, with no luck. The panic had started to churn in his stomach because Georgia would never have left Jessie or not answered his or the school's calls. When he phoned her work only to find she hadn't shown up that day, waves of panic started to hit him. Christy had taken Jessie from him while he'd gone to the police. That was an experience he would never forget either.

At first, they'd told him that Georgia needed to be missing for forty-eight hours before they could officially call Georgia missing. Lee knew the police captain, a friend of Lee's father, Captain Mike Drummond, and had insisted on talking to him. Mike had listened to Lee's story, and while he was talking to Mike, Georgia's car was found abandoned in a supermarket parking lot. There were no surveillance cameras around the shop or the parking lot, and no one remembered seeing Georgia.

That had truly surprised Lee because Georgia wasn't a woman that went unnoticed, and not because she was trying to attract attention. As hard as Georgia tried to blend in, her eyes, hair, and face made it impossible. Georgia was gorgeous and had a face that turned every head when she walked past. Her deep, rich red hair caught a person's attention, her startling jewel green eyes mesmerized them, and her smile bowled them over. Georgia always smiled. She had a big, compassionate heart, a gentle soul, and a brilliant mind.

When Georgia's car had been found with no trace of her, all the attention had turned to Lee. He immediately became the prime suspect in her disappearance. He'd even been suspended from work during the initial investigation because all eyes were on him. The investigation had gone on for over a year, but ten months into it, child protective services arrived at his house to take Jessie.

It was bad enough that his house had been turned upside down and every part of it gone over with a fine-tooth comb looking for evidence of foul play. Lee had also been grilled over and over again about the day Georgia went missing and the state of their marriage. They had investigated Lee's whole life; worse still, they dragged his family into it as well. The Young family's life became a fishbowl with people watching their every move. Lee's mother had tried to help him with the case, but Lee didn't want her any more involved than she already was. He was determined to defend himself, and he was a darn good defense attorney. But when child protective services came to his door because the school Jessie was going to lodged a concern with them, Lee knew he needed help. That's when he turned to Shaun Donovan and his well-known defense attorney father, Raymond Donovan.

The Donovans had taken over his case and had cleared Lee's name. They also got child protective services off Lee's back, and Jessie was taken out of the preschool she attended. The Donovans had found out that one of Jessie's teachers had been grilling a then three-year-old for information about Jessie's family. The teacher, who had only started at the school six months before Georgia went missing, was also the one who lodged the concern about Jessie.

The teacher had said Jessie had been withdrawn and scared every day she'd come to school after Georgia's disappearance. There were concerns about Lee neglecting Jessie as well and that the child was constantly left at school. The teacher had told child protective services that she could never get ahold of Lee. She had on more than one occasion had to call Lee's sister, Christy, to come and get Jessie. Over those harrowing eight to ten months after Georgia went missing, the police or FBI would randomly show up at Lee's house and drag him in for questioning. It was only on those occasions where Lee had not been able to get Jessie, but Lee had been the one to call Christy, not the teacher.

Once the Donovans had discredited the teacher and had subpoenaed her, the teacher had done her own disappearing act. There had been some speculation that Lee had been responsible for the teacher Mrs. Burns' disappearance as well. Only the police had managed to find out that Mrs. Burns wasn't her real name and that she was on the FBI's wanted list for matters they would not tell Lee or the Donovans. Mrs. Burns was one of the many people who'd randomly come into his life after that who wasn't who they claimed to be. That had made Lee suspicious that there was a lot more to Georgia's disappearance than he was being led to believe.

It was after the disappearance of Mrs. Burns that the U.S. Marshals suddenly became involved. Ty, Lee's cousin and the current Key West Police Captain, was with the U.S. Marshals back then. Ty was one of the special agents that were sent to Key West to take over the case. A case that was quickly and quietly put to bed once the Marshals had swooped in. Lee was told that Georgia's body had been found in a swamp near a small town outside of Miami. It was alleged that Georgia was taken because she'd stumbled upon a toxic waste dump site in the swamp, which was poisoning the small town's water supply.

The dumpsite had been making the residents sick, and Georgia had taken it upon herself to investigate it because she had a personal connection to one of the town's residents—a cousin of Georgia's who'd recently lost her child because of the poisoning. Georgia had used her resources at Key West Research Lab, where she'd been working, to test the water. The day Georgia had disappeared, she was going to meet with a U.S. Marshal who Ty had reached out to for her and that could help her. Only, Georgia hadn't shown up.

Hearing that Ty knew what had happened to Georgia from

day one had angered Lee, and he'd taken his emotions out on his cousin. Rationally, Lee knew that Ty couldn't tell Lee about an active investigation. Ty also wasn't the original agent on the case. So, Ty hadn't known a lot at the beginning and had only taken over the case after they'd allegedly found Georgia's body. Ty had to identify Georgia's body due to the special precaution that had to be taken with her body due to the nature of the toxic waste.

Lee hadn't even gotten to say goodbye to her, and instead of a body to bury, he'd been given a sealed urn with her ashes in it. After that, Lee had sold the house he and Georgia had lived in, along with everything in the house, and moved back home to Young House. Lee's father, Jake, had remodeled the one-bedroom cottage for Lee and Jessie into a sweet two-bedroom place with its own private yard and entrance. Not that the yard had remained private as Jessie grew older.... She loved being able to run around the huge backyard of the Young's house with her cousins.

Something had never sat right with Lee about the story the U.S. Marshals had given him. There were too many neatly patched-over holes. When he'd tracked down Georgia's cousin, Holly, her story had seemed rehearsed, and he could see in her eyes that she was scared. On more than one occasion after he'd met Holly, she'd tried to contact him, but before Holly could say anything to him, they'd been cut off.

The second time he'd gone to visit Holly, he'd found out that she and her husband had moved, and no one in the town knew where she'd gone. Holly, like Georgia, had vanished into thin air with not a single witness or anyone seeing. That had raised even more alarm bells for Lee and made him question whether the ashes he had in the urn on his mantle were Georgia's. That's when Lee started to dig more into the disappearance of his wife and had put even more strain on his already strained relationship with his cousin Ty.

Lee knew that if Georgia wasn't dead, and in his gut, he was sure she wasn't, there was only one agency that could make her disappear so well—the U.S. Marshals. Lee had hounded Ty and

Lee's younger brother, Justin, who was also in the U.S. Marshals by then, about it. But neither Ty nor Justin were any help and kept trying to convince Lee that Georgia was gone. This only fueled the need to find her, or at least the truth of what happened to her, even more, because never once did Ty or Justin refer to Georgia as dead. They would say Georgia was gone, and she wasn't coming back, ever.

Lee had also discovered through one of Georgia's close friends at Key West Labs that it was not water that Georgia had been testing but DNA samples. Lee also found out that Holly's baby had died at birth two years before Georgia started researching the supposed swamp water. Lee was led to believe that it had been a more recent event, and Georgia had been comparing Holly's baby's DNA to another child's DNA. But before he could find out anything more, all the research Lee had been given had disappeared from his office.

Lee hadn't given up and had tracked down every avenue his research had taken him. Then one day, Matty, Lee's youngest sister, was on assignment in a village in Africa when she swore she'd seen Georgia. Matty had questioned the villagers and shown them a picture she had on her phone of Georgia from before she'd disappeared. They had told Matty that the woman had been there. After further investigation, Matty found out that Georgia had been researching the high death rates of newborn babies in certain areas. Matty and her husband Johnathan started to help Lee and picked up on the story about the infant deaths while following the trail of the woman they thought was Georgia.

Although Matty never once blamed Lee, he'd always blamed himself for Johnathan's death. Johnathan was so deep into the story and was so close to finding the woman they thought was Georgia and what was actually going on when he was brutally murdered in Africa. By then, Matty was also deeply involved in the story, although she never revealed what she'd found. Two years after Jonathan's death, Matty had gone chasing after the truth behind her husband's death.

Matty had been gone for two years when she sent word that the woman who they'd been chasing wasn't Georgia but her doppelganger. Matty had told Lee that it was time to put Georgia to rest, and Georgia was researching why the babies had died to try and circumvent future deaths. That was when Lee had given up the thought that Georgia was alive. But he'd never given up trying to find out how she'd actually died and why. Lee knew Matty knew more than she was telling him. But, four years after Matty left on her mission, she too had disappeared and cut all ties with her family.

The only reason they knew or had hoped Matty was alive was by the odd email she sent every now and then to let the family know she was okay. The sad thing was that Matty had left her five-year-old daughter behind with their sister Christy. Hannah, Matty's daughter, now called Christy mom and never spoke about Matty.

Lee pinched the bridge of his nose. His obsession with finding out about Georgia had damaged his family, and after seeing a flash of red hair, he was once again obsessing about Georgia. Lee was going to go straight to Ty when he was done with Shaun to find out if he knew anything about the secret woman in Shaun's office. Lee had even thought about grilling Luke later on, as he would know, having been in the meeting with Shaun.

Lee needed to get a grip on himself. He wasn't going to go down this path again because of another Georgia look-a-like. He looked at his watch. Shaun was now almost twenty minutes late for their meeting. Lee was about to get up and reschedule when June ran back into the office and shut the door.

"Sorry, but the client is leaving, so all staff has to move into the break room once again," June explained. "They should just put a bag over the lady's head." She grinned at Lee, who shook his head at that suggestion.

"She's a client, not a criminal," Lee said.

"Well, we don't know that for sure," June reminded Lee just as Shaun walked into the room.

June excused herself and left.

"Hello, Lee," Shaun greeted him. "I'm sorry to have kept you waiting, but my meeting ran longer than I expected."

"That's okay," Lee told Shaun. "I see you were all closed up in the boardroom. Do you have another celebrity case?" he pried.

"Yes, something like that," was all Shaun would say about his client, and that brought the subject to the reason Lee was there to see him—to discuss Lee possibly taking over Donovan Law.

While Shaun spoke, Lee's mind ticked over coming up with a plan to find out who the woman Shaun and Luke were speaking to was.

Chapter Three

THE DANCE STUDIO

icky's heart beat with excitement as she turned the key in the lock to her new dance studio. She'd collected the keys from the real estate agent a couple of hours ago. She now owned the entire building. Vicky closed her eyes and took a deep breath as she pushed the door open. It was like a dream for her to own the dance studio where she'd learned to dance. Vicky had been dancing since the age of four. She slowly opened her eyes and stepped into the reception room.

The blinds were drawn, so the room was not as bright as it usually was with its large one-way glass windows that looked out onto the historic Duval Street in Old Town. You could find almost anything at any hour on Duval Street and the streets that led off of it. Vicky opened the blinds that were covering the windows and let the sunlight spread its rays and fill the room.

Vicky did a twirl around the room as she took it all in. All of Mrs. Amelia's current students were staying on, and Vicky expected to get even more students of more diverse age groups. She was going to be adding ballroom and Latin dancing, hip-hop, and ballet to Mrs. Amelia's modern dance classes. Mrs. Amelia once offered both ballet and modern dance with some ballroom dancing in the evenings. But over the years, she was finding it harder to cope, so she'd closed down two of the four dance studios in her building.

Vicky walked through to the main studio and opened the door. As expected, the floor and mirrors shone and as with the other studios, Mrs. Amelia had given Vicky a building certificate stating the floors were still in excellent condition. According to the realtor, Mrs. Amelia had the entire dance studio revamped not more than three years ago. Vicky walked into the room and couldn't resist a twirl at one of the bars in front of the mirrors. Before she could move over to look at the piano, she heard the front doorbell ring.

Vicky looked at her wristwatch and smiled. Of course, her recruits would be on time for their new assignments. Vicky picked up the purse she'd put on the floor before having a twirl at the bar and walked through to the reception area, freezing when she saw the silhouette framed in the frosted glass of the front door.

"What is he doing here?" Vicky muttered to herself with a frown creasing her brows.

Vicky unlocked and pulled open the front door to come face to face with Lee Young.

"I hope you're not here for dance lessons because we're not opening until next week." Vicky grinned up at Lee, whose six-foot-four frame dwarfed Vicky's by at least seven inches.

"Hello to you too," Lee greeted her, handing her a bunch of yellow roses with a card on it. "This is a *congratulations on your dance studio'* bouquet."

"Thank you," Vicky took the flowers. "They are beautiful. But something tells me you didn't come all this way to give me a dance studio warming gift."

"I see you're still as sharp as you always were!" Lee looked down at her with raised eyebrows. "Do you mind if I come in?"

"Oh!" Vicky laughed, realizing she was still blocking the doorway with Lee standing outside. "Come on in." She stood back for Lee to walk inside. "I hope you haven't been turned into a vampire over the years, and I've just given you carte blanche to enter my premises whenever you wish to make my studio your personal snack bar."

Vicky walked over to the reception desk and placed the flowers on it before pointing towards the waiting room chairs for Lee to take a seat.

"Please don't tell me you're still obsessed with vampires and werewolves!" Lee rolled his eyes as he unbuttoned his suit jacket and took a seat.

"Does one ever get over their obsession with fantasy?" Vicky grinned and sat down in a chair opposite him. "But my dark mind aside, what brings you to my part of the world?"

"I know you've only just got back to Key West, and I hate imposing on you, but I have a favor to ask of you," Lee told her.

"Okay..." Vicky's eyes narrowed. "Does this have anything to do with Jessie and...." She clicked her fingers as she pretended to think of his girlfriend's name. "Sally... No. Samantha?"

Lee sighed and shook his head, "No, it doesn't." He looked at her and frowned. "Why would you think the favor was about Jessie and Samantha?"

"Oh... no, nothing!" Vicky waved it off. "Forget I even asked that. What is this favor?"

"There it is again!" Lee's eyes narrowed as his eyes seemed to bore through Vicky as if he was trying to read her mind.

"There, what is again?" Vicky gave Lee a sideways look.

"That look!" Lee pointed at her. "You had that same look on your face when you were talking to Samantha last night," he pointed out. "I could've sworn you'd recognized Samantha when you saw her and were introduced."

"I think you're imagining things," Vicky had forgotten how astute Lee was. Being able to quickly assess and read people was what made Lee an excellent lawyer. "I was just surprised to see you were with someone and had brought her to a family dinner."

"No." Lee shook his head as he eyed Vicky. "It was more than that."

"Seriously, Lee, I do not know Samantha, nor have I met her before," Vicky was careful to say. "I think you're feeling a little insecure about what's going through the family's mind about her. So, you're being a little touchy about Samantha because of it."

"So what? You're a psychologist now?" Lee asked her as he sat back.

"I could be," Vicky teased him. "You never know what I've been up to since living in Miami for all these years."

"I think, as you and my sister are still tight as ever, that I have a pretty good idea," Lee grinned. "About my favor...."

"I'm all ears," Vicky told him. "You know I'll always try and find a way to help a Young."

"Vicky, do you still have contacts at the agency?" Lee came straight out and asked her. "I know you retired when Grant got ill, but I was hoping you still had connections."

"Why?" Vicky was not expecting Lee to ask that.

"You know you went above and beyond for me when Georgia went missing," Lee said softly. "I'll never forget that. If it weren't for what you were able to give us, Matty, Jonathan, and I would never have discovered what we did."

"Of course," Vicky said passionately. "We all cared about Georgia and you and Jessie. I wish I could've done more and found out everything you wanted to know for you."

"You gave us more information than anyone else did," Lee assured her.

"I thought you'd stopped looking into Georgia's disappearance after what happened to Johnathan," Vicky looked at Lee intently. "Why the sudden interest again?"

"Can I be honest with you?" Lee leaned forward again. "I never really stopped looking into Georgia's disappearance and alleged death."

"I didn't think you had," Vicky admitted. "To be honest, neither did I."

"Oh?" Lee looked at her, surprised.

"Every opportunity I got, I would sneak a look into her case file, hoping to find some sort of update," Vicky told him.

"Georgia left a giant-sized hole in all our lives," Lee said.

"Did they ever catch the agent they thought was the mole that had tipped the company off about Georgia's research?"

"I'm not sure," Vicky's stomach clenched, and she had to stop her jaw and hands from doing so as well. That agent Lee had referred to was another of the reasons Vicky had taken this assignment. "What's this about, Lee?" She steered the conversation away from the agent Lee had brought up.

"I had a meeting with your father this morning. He wanted to discuss me taking over Donovan Law," Lee explained. "When I was there, I saw a woman in the boardroom that looked like Georgia."

"Are you sure?" Vicky's brows creased. "Did you ask my father?"

"No," Lee shook his head. "Not even your father's staff knew who she was as she'd been escorted in by a U.S. Marshal, and the boardroom had been shut up tight until she left."

"How did you manage to get a look at her?" Vicky asked curiously.

"There was a gap in the blinds, and I managed to take a small look." Lee grinned. "I was wondering what all the secrecy was as your father usually has this open-door policy."

"And you're sure the woman looked like Georgia?" Vicky asked Lee once again.

"Well, from behind, she definitely did," Lee said. "The hair color, the way she sat, and the way she flicked her hair." His brows furrowed.

"Lee, you saw the woman from behind," Vicky pointed out.

"I'm telling you, Vicky, it was Georgia," Lee said emphatically. "I know it sounds crazy, and I can't explain it, but I just know it was her."

"Okay, well, let me reach out and see what I can find," Vicky promised him. "If all else fails, we can go to Plan B."

"Oh, no!" Lee shook his head wide-eyed. "I've never liked your Plan Bs."

"That's because you were always such a freakin' goody-two-shoes always wanting to do everything the right way." Vicky rolled her eyes. "Sometimes, you have to get your hands dirty to get what you want." She grinned. "Do you remember Shannon at that ballroom dancing competition that year you and Sarah-Lou went up against Shannon and James?"

"How can I forget that?" Lee shook his head. "I broke my ankle and lost my middle school sweetheart and dance partner."

"You were better off without Sarah-Lou. She was holding you back in ballroom dancing," Vicky told him with a cheeky grin. "I don't think Sarah-Lou ever danced again after that. She looked like Fred Flintstone peddling his car at top speed as her feet took off on that grease Shannon had put on the floor."

"Shannon had no qualms about getting her hands dirty to get what she wanted." Lee laughed. "If I remember, after all that fierce competition between Shannon and I over the junior ball-room dancing championship, neither of us took home the trophy that year."

"Nope, Shannon was disqualified, and so were you for swearing at her," Vicky reminded him.

"I didn't really swear at her. I just called her a female dog." Lee defended his actions. "Shannon broke my ankle!"

"Well, you should've rather said *'you female dog!'*" Vicky told him. "Then the judges might have let you back into the competition the next year when your ankle healed." She gave him a big grin. "Besides, Shannon didn't break your ankle. You would've been fine if you'd just let go of Sarah-Lou and let her speed off in her Fred-Flintstone car. But nooo, you had to be a hero and try to help her."

"Sarah-Lou was going to break something if I hadn't helped her," Lee pointed out.

"Instead, you ended up with the broken ankle," Vicky bit her bottom lip. "You couldn't even say you'd broken your ankle in a cool way. Sarah-Lou landed on your ankle and snapped it like a twig."

"What are you saying?" Lee's eyes narrowed. "I have brittle bones?"

"If the shoe fits…" Vicky teased him. "Have you done any ballroom dancing lately?"

"Heck, no," Lee looked disgusted. "I stopped dancing as soon as I hit my senior year."

"I know that, and that's not what I asked. Although can I just say that you quitting was a shame," Vicky told him earnestly. "You were one of the best ballroom dancers in Key West. Well, male dancers anyway."

"Thank you!" Lee said. "But please, for the love of saving face, please, can we never tell anyone outside of my family about my dancing days?"

"Ohhhh…" Vicky's eyes widened, and her eyebrows rose. "Your girlfriend doesn't know her boyfriend is the four-time junior state ballroom dance winner?"

"No," Lee said. "And I'd really like to keep it that way."

"Here I was hoping that you'd come to give my students a few lessons." Vicky sighed. "But don't worry, your secret is safe with me."

"That won't be happening," Lee assured her. "Besides, I haven't danced in years. I think the last time was at my wedding."

"That's such a shame," Vicky told him and then got distracted when the front doorbell chimed once again. "That must be my new employees."

"That's my cue to leave," Lee said, standing up as Vicky rushed past him.

"I'll let you know as soon as I have some information for you," Vicky told Lee. "Thanks for stopping by and considering what I said about giving my students some dance lessons."

"If I say I'll consider it, will you promise not to badger me about it?" Lee asked her as she stepped up to the front door.

"Nope!" Vicky shook her head. "I'll keep badgering you until you agree. How long have you known me for?" She gave him a smug smile. "You know I always get what I want in the end, and I don't have to grease the floor."

"I'll let you know when I've decided," Lee told her.

Vicky opened the door to four people standing on the doorstep with a tall, exceptionally good-looking dark-haired man about to ring the bell again.

"There you are!" the man said with a distinctly Latin American accent.

"I should've known it would be you, Dante, getting impatient and double ringing the doorbell," Vicky gave the incredibly good-looking man a cool look.

"You're not going to try and give me another lesson in patience, are you?" Dante looked pained. "I hate your lessons. They are like endless torture, and I would rather have a hot poker stuck in my eye."

"I'm glad to see I'm not the only one Vicky loves to torture," Lee grinned at the look Vicky gave him. "I'm Lee Young." He held out his hand.

"Dante Alverez, new studio manager and Latin dance teacher," Dante said and shook Lee's hand. "This is our ballerina, Robin Kelly, and her son Oliver Kelly."

"And I'm Cory Alverez," another young woman stepped up from behind Dante. "New receptionist, PA, and the hip hop or alternative style dance teacher."

"Hi," Lee greeted them all.

Vicky noticed Lee's frown as he looked at Robin and Oliver. Before he could ask what Vicky knew he was going to ask next, she maneuvered Lee out the door and her four new staff members into the studio.

"Once again, Lee, thanks for stopping by and the flowers," Vicky said amidst her staff, telling Lee it was nice to meet him.

"Is it just me, or are you suddenly eager to get rid of me?" Lee looked at her suspiciously. "Are you and...?" He raised his eyebrows.

"What?" Vicky looked at Lee confused at first until it dawned on her he was implying that she and Dante were an item. "Me and Dante?" She nearly choked. "Oh, no!" She shook her head. "You know what a flirt Justin is?" She used Lee's younger brother as an example. "Well, Dante is about two hundred times worse than Justin."

"Great," Lee gave a low whistle. "Let's hope Key West is big enough for both of their egos."

Vicky and Lee said their goodbyes before Lee walked around the corner where Vicky assumed he was going to the parking lot.

"So that's Lee Young?" Robin's voice made her jump.

The woman was like a ninja and needed to wear a bell around her neck.

"Yes, that's Lee Young," Vicky confirmed. "As soon as I've got Dante and Cory settled into the apartment upstairs, I'll take you and Oliver to the house I've rented near mine."

"What is the house called again?" Robin asked her.

"It doesn't really have a name, but it has this small willow grove in front of it which protects the house from the wind off the sea," Vicky told her. "The house has a lot of history, which I thought you'd like. It's been in the Shaw family for generations. Most of the Shaws have moved away from Key West, and the house usually stands open."

"I loved the photographs you sent of the house and how the family has remodeled the inside of it," Robin smiled excitedly. "I can't wait to get settled in, and it's close to...."

"I love the apartment upstairs," Cory came bounding back into the reception, interrupting Robin's sentence. "Thank you so much for giving me this opportunity, Vicky." She hugged Vicky.

"You deserved it," Vicky assured Cory. "I'll show you the side entrance, which is a private entrance into the apartment. It also has a secluded backyard."

Vicky showed Cory, Dante, Oliver, and Robin around the studio and then the three-bedroom apartment that occupied the third story of the building. Once Cory and Dante were comfortable and off to stock up the apartment, Vicky took Robin and Oliver to the Shaw house, which was one street over from Vicky's family home and shared Union Beach with the other four houses on Vicky's street.

When they pulled up, they were greeted by Tarryn Young, Lee's cousin and Ty Young's sister.

"Aunt Tarryn," Oliver greeted Tarryn with a hug. "It's good to see you. How is Holden?"

"He's recovering," Tarryn told him. "Thank goodness my cousin's daughter is a doctor."

Vicky, Tarryn, and Robin watched Oliver take a box inside the house before they continued their conversation.

"Hi, Tarryn," Robin hugged Tarryn. "How are you holding up?"

"I'm fine," Tarryn told them. "I'll feel better once Holden is better and my mess is all cleaned up."

"I know," Robin put her arm around Tarryn's shoulder comfortingly. "We're here for you if you need us."

"Thanks," Tarryn gave them a small smile. "I was so glad when Vicky told me you were all coming to Key West last week." She swallowed nervously. "I hate living like this, and what's worse, I could be putting my family in danger. But I don't know what else to do. I have Holden to think about."

"You are right where you should be," Vicky assured Tarryn. "We're here now, so you can relax a little because we'll be keeping an eye on you."

"I best be getting back before I'm seen here," Tarryn said, looking back over her shoulder. "I'll pop by later with Holden. We've started walking on the beach in the early evening."

"We'll be here," Robin promised.

Tarryn gave them all a hug and disappeared as quietly as she'd appeared.

"Oliver," Vicky looked at the strapping young man who was in his late twenties. He was walking back towards them to grab another box out of Robin's car. "I hear you've got a job at Key West Research Facility?"

"Yes, I have," Oliver said to her. "I start on Monday."

"A friend of mine's daughter is also working there," Vicky told him.

"I was lucky to get in," Oliver said. "But I'm very happy that

I did. KW Research Facility is a leader in many fields, including genetics.”

“I believe they are,” Vicky said. “It certainly gives any young geneticist an edge in their career.”

“I’ve rented Oliver a car until we can buy him one, and it gets delivered tomorrow,” Robin told Vicky. “I’ve asked Dante to come and check it out. You never know if there’s anything wrong with it or not.”

“Mom,” Oliver sighed and shook his head. “You know I know exactly what you mean when you speak in your agent code.” He rolled his eyes. “Please, just say that Dante is going to sweep the car for bugs or tracking devices and then plant a few of his own.”

“I would never violate your privacy like that,” Robin looked shocked that Oliver would even suggest such a thing. “But Dante will sweep the car, and we don’t need to place anything in your car.” She gave him a smug smile.

“Great!” Oliver threw his hands in the air before walking off to collect another box.

“Are you sure you’re okay to be here with everything going on with your brother?” Vicky looked at Robin worriedly after Oliver walked off.

“I need to be here because of that!” Robin assured Vicky. “And I need to be here for Tarryn. I know she thinks she can handle this....”

“We just have to make sure Tarryn’s prepared for what’s to come once we find him,” Vicky bit her bottom lip. “Let’s hope we can put this behind us once and for all after that.”

“You know, Vicky, all I want to do is to teach ballet again and enjoy my retirement with my son.” Robin sighed and looked out at the sea. “I could get used to this, being here. I want to be here. I want to buy this place and settle down.”

“Well, you have the first option on it,” Vicky told Robin with an encouraging smile. “Look, you are going to have this. We both are. But we need to do this one last mission.”

“I know,” Robin said.

“Now, let me help you move in and show you around.” Vicky

put her arm through Robin's and turned her towards the house. As Vicky and Robin walked into the house, Vicky felt a tingle down her spine—they were being watched.

"You feel that too, right?" Robin said softly.

Vicky nodded. They stepped inside as if they hadn't noticed.

"Where have you been?" The man's cold blue eyes assessed him. "Or should I take a guess?"

"I know!" The man's golden brown eyes were shadowed and guarded. "But this thing is dragging out, and all I want to do is get back to my family."

"Look, although it might not seem like it, I do understand how you feel," the blue-eyed man told him. "But you've got to lie low. I took a big risk by letting you crash here. Trust me; my position is a lot worse than yours." He walked into the cramped kitchen and pulled a bottle of amazingly fine whisky from a cabinet along with two glasses. "You have to trust the person who is helping you. I promise you they are doing everything in their power to help you." He poured two glasses of the amber liquid and pushed one over.

"How can you be so trusting?" he asked the blue-eyed man that was about the same age as he was.

"Because your special agent in charge is helping me as well," the blue-eyed man sat down in the small breakfast booth. "What I can tell you is that the one person who helped me and kept me alive all this time is your special agent in charge."

"And how long have you been in hiding?" It was a rhetorical question. He knew exactly who he was boarding with and how long the man had been *disappeared* for.

"My situation is more complicated than yours," the blue-eyed man took a long swallow of the amber liquid.

"And how do you figure that?" He sat down and took the whisky.

"Because my situation involves the murder of a federal

deputy director," the blue-eyed man shocked him by saying. "I see that was information on me you didn't have."

The man held up his glass in a salute, "To the truth! May it be discovered soon and hopefully free us both!"

"To the truth!" he saluted with his glass of whisky. "May I be able to finally get back to my family and explain everything."

"I'll drink that as well!" The blue-eyed man held up his glass once again before downing the last drop. "I've put some fresh fish on the fire for dinner tonight. I hope you like fish."

He sat fiddling with the glass in front of him. His mind ticked over on how he could reach out to his family and explain things. He hated thinking what they must think of him and how they must see him as a traitor or an enemy of the country. Until he could find a way back to them, his new roommate was right. He needed to lie low and trust his S.A.C. He knew his S.A.C. was risking their own career by helping him lie low. But trust was not his strongest virtue, and neither was patience.

His stomach grumbled, reminding him that he hadn't eaten the entire day and that the fish cooking on the fire outside smelled really good. He downed the rest of the whisky and got up to find out when dinner was going to be ready.

Chapter Four

THE LAW OFFICE OPERATION

"Vicky, I'm not sure we should be doing this," Lee hissed, standing behind Vicky and nervously looking around the alley. "We could trip an alarm or get caught on camera."

"Geez, relax, man," Vicky looked back at Lee. "Besides, you look like a ninja covered head to toe in that black sweatsuit and balaclava outfit. No one would ever recognize you." She had had to bite her lip to stop from laughing at him.

"Very funny," Lee said, glaring at her. "You told me we were going to sneak into your father's office in the dead of night, so I dressed for the occasion." He looked at her outfit pointedly. "You also look like a burglar in your black gym pants and sweatshirt."

"Exactly," Vicky turned and indicated her outfit with an open hand. "I'm dressed like a burglar, not a ninja who lost his sword and nunchucks."

She turned back to the door and carefully popped it open.

"It's a Katana," Lee told her. "A ninja sword is called a Katana."

"Thanks!" Vicky said sarcastically, pulling a face at him before she dashed into the office and disarmed the alarm. "You can come inside now."

Lee slipped into the office behind her. "I seriously feel this is wrong on so many different levels."

"Look, it's this, or we nab Luke, shove him into the back of a van, take him to an undisclosed location and interrogate the information out of him," Vicky looked at Lee with raised eyebrows, waiting for his response.

"This isn't some black ops situation, and there'll be no interrogating my nephew," Lee told her sternly before stopping and looking at her with narrowed eyes. "I can't tell whether you were serious about interrogating Luke or just kidding."

"It's my excellent poker face," Vicky explained. "Of course, I was kidding. I'm not CIA!"

"Anymore!" Lee said under his breath.

"Excuse me?" Vicky looked at Lee.

"Nothing!" Lee shrugged.

"We have to get into my father's office," Vicky told Lee. "He keeps all his top-secret or highly sensitive cases locked in a safe behind that hideously large photo of his racehorse."

"I love that photo of Renegade," Lee told Vicky. "He was a great horse, and your father loved him."

"Yes, but he wasn't the greatest racehorse, was he?" Vicky shook her head and stopped in front of her father's office. She went through the set of keys she'd borrowed from her father to find his office key. "Here we go." She unlocked Shaun's office and stepped inside.

"Your father has a safe behind that picture of Renegade?" Lee looked at the large ceiling to floor picture of Shaun Donovan's horse in amazement. "Why have I only heard about this now?"

"I don't know," Vicky shrugged. "Christy and I used to have endless hours of fun pretending to be safe crackers and playing with my father's large safe."

"How do you move the picture?" Lee ran his hand down the side of the picture.

"Really?" Vicky moved behind Shaun's desk and shook her head at Lee. "My father would never have the button to the safe in the picture."

"Oh, is it one of the books on the bookshelf next to it?" Lee's eyes lit with excitement. He couldn't remember when last he'd had so much fun even though they were technically breaking and entering.

"This isn't some old-fashioned whodunnit!" Vicky sighed as Lee turned around to stare at her.

Vicky smiled at him and put her hand under the desk. There was a click, and the picture popped forward.

"Nice," Lee said, nodding his approval. "I think you've just sold me on taking over Donovan Law. If nothing else but for this cool safe."

Lee swung the large painting away from the wall and stood staring at a large safe door. "It's like a bank vault." He looked around at Vicky wide-eyed.

"Uh-huh," Vicky nodded before walking towards the safe and typing in the code. "Now comes the really fun part. I have no idea what my father's filing system is like."

Vicky had just opened the safe when she heard a noise and froze. She put her finger to her mouth and stepped around Lee. "Wait here," Vicky told him softly before walking towards the office door and peeking out.

They could hear voices: one male and one female. Vicky quietly closed and locked the office door before dashing over to her father's desk, where she fiddled with something beneath it before rushing back to where Lee was standing at the entrance to the vault.

"I hope you're not claustrophobic," Vicky said before shoving Lee into the vault, pulling the door shut, and hitting a lever.

"What the heck, Vicky!" Lee said through gritted teeth. "You've locked us in the vault."

"Would you rather be out there with whoever's just broken into my father's offices?" Vicky asked him.

"We just broke into your father's offices!" Lee pointed out. "What if they get into his safe and find us?"

"They won't," Vicky assured Lee. "Now, keep quiet!" She glared at him. "It's going to get dark in here."

"What?" Lee's brows furrowed together, and the world around them went black.

"Make sure your phone is on silent," Vicky said softly.

"It's always on silent," Lee told her.

"No buzzing either!" Vicky warned him.

"I hate that vibrating thing," Lee admitted. "I can't see anything."

Lee took a step forward and knocked into Vicky. His hands shot out and grabbed her arms to steady her and pulled her into him. "I'm so sorry. Are you okay?" Lee said into her ear.

"Y... yes," Vicky stuttered and lifted her head up towards him as he lowered his to hear her.

Their cheeks brushed, and he could feel her warm breath near his ear. His heartbeat kicked up a notch, and a memory of a stolen kiss in the middle of Wilhelmina's willow grove when they were teenagers flashed before him. A knocking noise on the wall pulled him out of his memory, and Vicky quietly stepped away from him, leaving Lee feeling strangely alone and like someone had taken something important away from him. He shook the feeling off when the knocking noise was heard once again.

"They're in my father's office," Vicky whispered. "Keep very still and move with me."

Vicky took Lee's arm and gently tugged him backward with her until they came up against a shelf.

"This part of the safe is where my father has some blankets that we need to cover ourselves with," Vicky told Lee.

"Why?" Lee asked her softly.

"In case they have thermal imaging devices," Vicky said, feeling along the shelves until she found one. "We're going to have to share a blanket."

Lee and Vicky dropped down onto the ground. Vicky was sitting right up against Lee's side. He put his arm around her and pulled her close to his side before covering them both with the blanket. Lee wasn't sure how long they sat there for, but it felt like hours, and what was worse, Lee was suddenly very aware of Vicky, as he had been all those years before he'd met Georgia.

Vicky had grown up at Lee's family home as she was Lee's younger sister Christy's lifelong best friend. Vicky was sassy, bold, and could dance rings around most people in many different dance forms including, modern, ballet, and ballroom. Vicky was also fiercely loyal to and protective over Christy. No one, not even Christy's twin sister, Shannon, would ever try to bully Christy with Vicky around. Her grandfather had been a champion mixed martial arts fighter and had taught Vicky how to defend herself from as young as four years old.

Vicky was always leading Christy on misadventures. Lee would have to pull them out of trouble, and nine times out of ten would end up in trouble for doing so. Where Christy was a thrill-seeker who loved extreme sports and trying out new adventures, Vicky was the one who sought out their next high adrenaline adventure. Between the two of them, Lee was sure he was going to be gray before he turned eighteen.

Up until the age of sixteen, Lee had always just seen Vicky as another annoying kid sister. Then one day, Lee was out running along the beach when he'd seen Vicky, who was fourteen at the time, run towards Wilhelmina's willow grove. She'd looked upset, so Lee had followed her to find out what was wrong.

When he stepped into the grove he saw Vicky sitting on the sand hugging her legs to her chest with tears streaming down her soft, smooth cheeks, his heart melted. Lee had sat down next to Vicky and tried to make her laugh before putting his arm around her and pulling her to his side. Much like they were sitting right now. Only back then, he'd let her have a good cry and pour her heart out to him. Vicky's mother had left Vicky and her father for another man when Vicky was eight. Not just any man but Manny Butler, who lived on the same block as they all did. Manny Butler was also Aaron Butler, Lee's best friend's father.

Manny moved with Belinda to his house in Miami after they'd gotten married. But Aaron stayed behind with his aunt to finish school in Key West. Every so often, Belinda and Manny would come home to visit Aaron for a couple of weeks. This was one of those weeks, and Vicky had seen her mother. As hard as

Vicky tried to make everyone think she didn't care about her mother or what she'd done, Lee had always known it cut her to the bone. This time, Belinda had taken it one step further and completely snubbed her daughter. Vicky had heard Manny ask Belinda if she'd seen Vicky, to which Belinda asked, "Who is Vicky?"

Eventually, Vicky had stopped crying and had made Lee swear he wouldn't tell anyone about her crying over the wicked witch. Lee had promised, and that was when their eyes had met and held. Lee's mind had gone blank of all rational thought, and his heart flipped over a few times as he noticed just how blue Vicky's eyes were and the smell of her magnolia shampoo. Before he knew what had happened, he was kissing her. At that moment, Lee knew that he'd fallen for Vicky and finally admitted to himself what Aaron had been pointing out to him for over a year. That Lee felt a lot more for Vicky than he'd even admit to himself.

Lee couldn't pinpoint the exact day he'd fallen for her. Or maybe he'd been in love with her since he was a kid. But Aaron and some of his other friends had noticed how angry he got if anyone mentioned Vicky as a potential date. Or how whenever she walked into a room, Lee would get lost as he watched her, and how he'd started to avoid being alone with her. But at that moment in the willow grove, he had to admit to himself that he was head over heels in love with his sister's beautiful, mischievous, sassy, and big-hearted friend.

When the kiss ended, Vicky had been mortified and had made Lee promise that they would never say a word to anyone, not even Christy, about this. But Lee hadn't agreed. He admitted to Vicky that he'd found himself developing feelings for her over the past year and that he might always have had feelings for her. Vicky had admitted that she'd had a giant crush on Lee for as long as she could remember, and that was why she refused to pair up with him for ballroom dancing. It hadn't been that Vicky hated ballroom dancing; she couldn't dance with Lee for fear he'd find out she had a crush on him.

But no matter how Vicky had felt about Lee, she valued her friendship with Christy, and the Young family was her family. Vicky didn't want to jeopardize that if their relationship went sour, and even though her heart wanted to reach out to him, her mind knew it was best for them to remain friends. That's when she'd asked Lee not to hate her. She said he was her first love, but Vicky knew first hand first love hardly ever ended well, and she valued him as a big brother figure and never wanted to lose that.

Instead of her honesty making him angry, it had made him fall even more in love with her. For a fourteen-year-old, Vicky saw the world through adult eyes. It was also after that day Lee had become even more protective over Vicky. He'd understood where she was coming from because of what her mother had done to her and her dad. Lee was determined that no one would ever hurt Vicky in the same way. Even while Vicky was at university, Lee would keep an eye on her even though he was with Georgia at the time.

When Vicky met Grant, Lee had insisted on meeting him and had stayed an entire weekend with Grant and Vicky in New York to make sure Grant was right for her. It was during that weekend that Lee knew Grant was as madly in love with Vicky as Lee was with Georgia. Grant had told Lee that weekend how he felt about Vicky. Grant and Lee had become close friends over the years. When Grant became ill, Lee often went to Miami to help him and Vicky. Before Grant died, he'd made Lee promise to always keep looking out for Vicky, no matter what. Lee wasn't quite sure what the *no matter what* implied, but Lee assured Grant that he'd always be there for both of them.

When Grant had died, Vicky started withdrawing into her shell, and she pushed Lee away, asking him to please give her space. Then Lee had met Samantha, and his time was spread thin between Jessie in Boston, his job, and Samantha in Key West. Lee was sad to admit that until Vicky had come home, he hadn't seen her in a good fourteen months.

"Hey!" Vicky's voice penetrated his thoughts. "When you're done snoring, I think whoever was in the office has gone."

"Great, because my butt is numb from this hard floor," Lee grumbled.

Lee pushed the blanket off them and stood up. Before he could offer Vicky a hand, she'd sprung to her feet and switched on the flashlight on her phone. Vicky walked towards the vault door and found the emergency open button that was there in case anyone accidentally got locked in the safe.

Lee looked at the safe door expecting it to pop open, but it didn't. He looked at Vicky questioningly.

"No, don't tell me I accidentally hit the panic switch!" Vicky's eyes traveled to the wall. "I hit the panic switch." She swiveled and stared up at Lee. "Shoot!"

"What does that mean?" Lee gave her a sideways look.

"That we're trapped in here for six hours!" Vicky looked at him apologetically.

"No!" Lee immediately walked to the wall and tried the button Vicky had hit once again. "Why would Shaun install something like this in his office?"

"Because of the sensitive cases he takes on," Vicky explained to Lee. "He had to have this installed to keep the case files and various sensitive information in."

"I have court in a couple of hours, and I have to be there," Lee told her. "We have to get out of here, Vicky."

"I'm already on it." Vicky scrolled through her phone and sent an S.O.S to someone, but he couldn't see who. It didn't take long for her to reply. "Help is on its way." She smiled up at him.

"While we wait, should we look for what we came here to find?" Lee suggested.

"While you were having forty winks, I already did," Vicky reached into her sweatshirt and pulled out a folder.

"You can't take that entire folder. Shaun will know it's missing," Lee told her.

"Shaun has a photocopying machine in here," Vicky shone her light into the far corner. "Trust me. If you do come on board to Donovan Law, you're going to find they do a lot more than first meets the eye. Because of the cases they are assigned, Shaun has this setup."

Lee's eyes widened when Vicky shone a light on the three desks with computer systems on them. "Wow!" He gave a low whistle. "You are making this very hard for me to turn this job down."

"What?" Vicky looked at Lee in surprise. "You're not going to take my father up on his offer?"

"I have a lot on my plate right now." Lee ran his hand through his hair. "Jessie has just moved back home, and things with Samantha are getting serious." His eyes met Vicky's. "I'm not sure how Samantha and Jessie are going to take me leaving the DA's office."

"Have you asked them?" Vicky raised her eyebrows.

"Well, I sort of mentioned leaving the DA's to Samantha when Shaun first put the offer on the table," Lee admitted. "She was shocked and hurt that I would think of leaving the place where we worked together."

"If your relationship with Samantha is getting serious," Vicky said, "wouldn't it be better for both of you if you didn't have to see each other twenty-four-seven? I hear that's really tough on a relationship."

"I didn't look at it like that," Lee nodded. "I'll talk to her and Jessie later on today if we ever get out of Fort Knox."

"Personally, Lee," Vicky gave him a small smile. "I think you'd be a fool to turn this opportunity down. It's not every day you get handed an established law firm on a golden platter. The reason my father offered you the firm is because he trusts you and respects you as much as he did your mother."

"I..." Lee swallowed, and his eyes widened at what Vicky had just told him. "Wow! I never once saw myself as half the lawyer my mother was, or your father is. That's quite the compliment."

"Well, don't let it go to your head," Vicky told him. "There are already two big heads in your family, and I don't think Ty or

Justin would appreciate more competition in the big ego department."

"Don't worry... there's no chance of that." Lee laughed. "I feel more humbled by what you said than anything else. But you're right. I've always wanted to work at Donovan Law side by side with my mother and your father."

"Well, my father is handing you that dream," Vicky pointed out. "Trust me, your mother may not be here physically, but she'll still be walking these halls with you every day."

"Thank you, Vicky," Lee said softly. "I think I needed to hear that in order to remember what my goals have been. You're right. This is what I've worked for my entire career."

"Exactly," Vicky said. "And, you're not married or even engaged to Samantha yet, and even if you were, if she really loved you, she'd never stand in your way of achieving your goals."

Before Lee could answer, the vault door hissed open. Lee and Vicky swung around to come face to face with his nephew Luke.

"You do know I should report the both of you for breaking and entering!" Luke's eyes narrowed, and he crossed his arms over his chest as he eyed Vicky and Lee.

"Technically, we didn't break in because I have keys to the office," Vicky pointed out before stepping up and leaning towards Luke to whisper something in his ear.

Lee watched Luke's eyes widen before he stepped back and glared at Vicky, "Oh, that is so unfair, and I think it is called blackmail."

"Or extortion, whichever works for you," Vicky patted Luke on the chest and smiled at him smugly before looking at her phone. "Let me see where Christy's number is?"

"Okay!" Luke held up his hands. "You know I would never have reported you. I was joking."

"I don't know what's going on here," Lee said, looking from Luke to Vicky. "But I think we need to get out of the office before we're really caught."

"I was only joking too," Vicky gave Luke a peck on his cheek. "I would never betray my favorite godson."

"Your only godson." Luke pointed out. "Should I call the police, though?" He stepped aside so Lee and Vicky could step out of the vault before shutting it and locking the picture in place. "You said you heard someone else in the office."

"Did you come in the front or back door?" Vicky asked Luke.

"I came through the front door in case anyone saw me," Luke told her. "I didn't want to draw suspicion."

"Clever," Vicky said. "Was the lock jimmied or the alarm off?"

"No," Luke shook his head. "The alarm was on, and there was no sign of forced entry. I also checked the alley door where you said you'd come into the office. It was all locked up and secure."

"My father has hired security guards that come into the office to check on it, has he?" Vicky asked Luke.

"No," Luke shook his head. "Not that I know of."

"What are you thinking?" Lee looked at Vicky.

"That it was someone who works for Uncle Shaun that is probably looking for the same information on our client that you both were!" Luke tapped his chin thoughtfully.

"How did you know that...?" Lee looked accusingly at Vicky.

"Don't look at me," Vicky told Lee. "I never said a word to Luke about why we were here."

"I kinda figured you'd somehow try and get information on the woman who was in the office when you came to see Uncle Shaun," Luke explained to Lee. "I've been waiting for you to question me about it."

"So, your client is Georgia?" Lee's eyes widened, and his heart skipped a few beats.

"You know I can't tell you that," Luke said apologetically. "But I'm sure the file Vicky made a copy of will give you a few clues."

"How did you...?" Vicky's eyes narrowed on Luke.

"I know you're in good shape, Aunt Vicky," Luke pointed to Vicky's torso. "But no one has flat square abs."

"Busted!" Vicky grinned.

"Just do me a favor," Luke told them. "Burn that file once you've looked it over."

"I will, I promise," Vicky promised Luke.

"Thank you," Luke said. "Now get out of here before we have some serious explaining to do to Uncle Shaun."

"Right!" Vicky nodded and headed for the door.

"Thanks, Luke," Lee smiled at his nephew.

"You can thank me by accepting Uncle Shaun's offer," Luke told Lee. "We need you here, Uncle Lee, especially now."

"What do you mean?" Lee's brow creased into a frown.

"There is a reason I'm letting you take that file," was all Luke would say. "Now, you'd better go."

Lee's mind was filled with questions about what Luke had just said as he followed Vicky out of the office. Lee had a dreadful feeling he was about to go down a path that was going to rock his entire life.

Chapter Five

ALL THE FUSS ABOUT OLIVER

"I haven't even had a chance to breathe yet," Vicky said into her phone as she let herself into her dance studio. "I'll let you know as soon as I've got the code cracked."

"Why is it even coded?" Lee's voice on the other end of the line was fraught with irritation. "What do you think Luke meant when he said there's a reason I'm letting you take that file?"

"Wait!" Vicky greeted Cory, who was already working on her laptop behind the reception desk. "What did Luke say to you?"

Lee repeated what he'd just said, "Why do you ask that?"

"Shoot!" Vicky swore under her breath, closed her eyes, and pinched the bridge of her nose. "We were played like a fine fiddle."

"What are you talking about?" Lee asked her.

"I've got to go," Vicky told Lee. "Can you meet me for lunch?"

"Oh..." Lee hesitated. "I was actually going to go ring shopping."

Vicky froze, and her eyes widened as tiny waves and shock stung her fingertips and zipped through her veins. "A ring?"

"Yes, I thought about what you said, and you're right," Lee told her. "It's time I started realizing all my goals. One of them happens to be to settle down with someone I love and trust and who is my best friend."

"I see," Vicky said. "Are you sure that Samantha is all those things to you and that you are not just seeing what you want to see in her?"

"That's an odd thing to say!" Lee told her.

"And have you spoken to Jessie about this yet?" Vicky asked Lee.

"Sort of," Lee said hesitantly. "Jessie just wants me to be happy, so I'm sure she'll be thrilled. I think she really likes Samantha."

"Well, I wish you the best of luck, Lee," Vicky's voice was a little hoarse. She cleared her throat. "I have to go. I have a lot of work to do, which also includes decrypting this file for you."

"Call me when you have something," Lee said quickly.

"Sure," Vicky hung up without saying goodbye.

Vicky's hands were shaking when she went to slip her phone back into her pocket.

"Are you okay, Vicky?" Cory looked at her worriedly. "You look a little gray. Did you get some shocking news?"

"I did!" Vicky told her, walking towards the reception desk. "Cory, how good are you with ciphers?"

"Excellent," Cory told her. "Why? Do you have a cipher for me to crack?"

"I do," Vicky said, handing Cory the file as an idea dawned on her. "I have to go out, Cory." She looked down at the file she'd just given Cory. "Will you see if you can make sense of the information in here? And this is between you and me." Before Vicky walked away, she said. "You won't forget to phone our current dance students to let them know our grand opening is in two weeks, will you?"

"I'm nearly finished going through the list," Cory told Vicky. "I've also nearly finished the ad, billboard poster, new website, and flyers."

"You are an absolute star!" Vicky told her. "I'm on my phone if you need me."

"Not to worry. I've got the office and this covered," Cory assured Vicky, pointing to the file.

Vicky ran out the front door when her new lunch date messaged back to say she could meet Vicky. If Vicky were going to help Lee, she would need to enlist the help of someone close to him, and Vicky knew just the person to help her with her plan. It was a plan that Vicky didn't really want to do. But she was running out of options, and if this latest plan didn't work, Vicky was going to have to stoop to a level she wasn't comfortable with.

"Aunt Vicky," Jessie stood up and waved so Vicky could see her sitting in a secluded booth at the corner coffee shop.

"Hi," Vicky walked up to the booth and sat down. "Thank you for meeting me for lunch."

"I'm glad you called," Jessie admitted. "I was thinking of popping into the dance studio. I would love to take dance lessons, and Luke tells me that you're offering more than just modern dance."

"That's right," Vicky confirmed. "I've tried to coax your father into coming to teach a few ballroom lessons."

"I don't think my father has danced since before he met my mother," Jessie laughed.

"I hear you may have a new addition to your family soon," Vicky said innocently.

"A new addition?" Jessie's brows furrowed. "I don't understand."

"Yes, you know, Samantha! Your father stood me up for lunch today to go ring shopping instead." Vicky picked up the menu and shook her head. "And I needed his help to try to figure out a cipher."

"Hold up," Jessie said, putting her hand on Vicky's menu and moving it down so Jessie could see Vicky's face. "First, my father is useless at crossword puzzles and wouldn't know the first thing about a cipher. I'm the better bet at helping you there," she told Vicky. "And what do you mean my father is going ring shopping?" she sputtered, her green eyes glittered with angry sparks.

"Oh, no...." Vicky dropped the menu dramatically and reached over to touch Jessie's hand comfortingly. "You didn't know?" Her face crumpled in despair. "Oh, dear... this is bad!" Her brows furrowed, and she hoped her face reflected her horror in having slipped up. "Please don't let your father know I told you. I think I've already got him into enough trouble for one day!"

"Wait..." Jessie closed her eyes and shook her head for a second before she looked at Vicky in confusion. "What is going on, Aunt Vicky?" She looked at Vicky expectantly. "I know my dad is up to something. Please tell me it doesn't have anything to do with my mother again!"

"Uh..." Vicky bit her lip and looked around the restaurant. "Where are all the waiters?"

"Aunt Vicky!" Jessie said. "Please, I need to know what is going on." She looked imploringly at Vicky. "I also wasn't only coming to the dance studio to sign up for dance lessons. I need your help with something."

"My help?" Vicky looked at Jessie, her brows furrowing.

Jessie looked around the room to make sure they were still secluded. She leaned forward on the table and said softly, "Aunt Vicky, there is something you should know."

"Okay!" Vicky felt little alarm bells ringing in her head.

Jessie reached inside her bag and pulled out a folder, which she handed to Vicky.

"Where did you get this, Jessie?" Vicky's eyes were wide with shock. "You shouldn't have information like this."

"Sorry, Aunt Vicky, I wanted to show you this the other night, but Aunt Christy didn't let you out of her sight, and that grapevine that was clinging to Dad's arm had you in her crosshairs," Jessie explained.

"Jessie, you shouldn't have this information," Vicky said

softly, grabbing a breadstick as she leaned forward on the table. "Where did you get this information from?"

"You don't need to be in the FBI to have contacts," Jessie told her.

"Jessie, if you're caught with this information," Vicky pointed to the file. "You'll be in a lot of trouble or more likely a federal prison for stealing records from the DA's office." Her eyes narrowed. "What are you up to and why do you have this information?"

"I will tell you!" Jessie looked at Vicky. "But you have to promise not to tell my father or Aunt Christy."

"You know I can't promise that," Vicky told her honestly. "If your life is in danger, Jess, and I didn't tell them...."

"Well, then I can't tell you what I'm up to," Jessie sat back and crossed her arms over her chest, looking at Vicky defiantly.

"Fine!" Vicky relented. "But know this, if I feel you are in even the teeniest bit of danger, I will tell your father."

"Fair enough," Jessie agreed to those terms. "But I also want to know why my father pulled out all the old files he had on my mother's disappearance?"

"He did that?" Vicky's brows drew together.

"Yes," Jessie told her.

"That's because your father is convinced he saw your mother in my father's boardroom the other day," Vicky explained to Jessie.

"Was it her?" Jessie's eyes had that same spark of hope Vicky had seen in Lee's eyes.

"I'm not sure, but I doubt it, honey," Vicky gave Jessie an encouraging smile. "Your mother isn't coming back, Jess. If your father has pulled out his investigation research on her disappearance, then he's even deeper than I at first thought."

"In my head, I know that my mother's gone," Jessie's eyes darkened with emotion. "But in my heart, there's still this little pocket of hope that refuses to be closed or filled by anything else," she admitted to Vicky. "I know I'm always telling my father he has to stop seeing her everywhere. But the truth is, I do the exact same thing. My breath catches in my throat and my heart races every time I see someone who remotely resembles her or has the exact same hair color as hers.”

“I think that seeing your mother everywhere you go is a sign that she’s still with you in your heart,” Vicky said softly. “When you were little, you once told me that you carried her around in a special pocket in your heart.” She grinned. “Now I understand what you mean by that.” She gave Jessie’s hand a comforting squeeze. “And you know no matter how dark or bad life gets, you have a little piece of her sunshine warming you from the inside.”

“Aunt Vicky, what did you mean my father’s in a lot deeper than you thought?” Jessie steered the conversation back to her father.

“I think your father is getting cold feet with his relationship with Samantha,” Vicky explained. “That’s probably why he’s going to shop for a ring because he wants to believe that he can settle down with someone again. I also think that’s probably why he thought whoever was in my father’s office looked like Georgia.”

“That’s another reason I wanted to speak to you, Aunt Vicky,” Jessie looked up when the waiter appeared at their table. “Hi, Leo.” She greeted the young man. “Why is service so slow today?” she teased him, making him blush.

“Sorry, Jess,” Leo said. “My father is not well, and I’m here running the place on my own as my mother has gone to get him medication.”

“I’m sorry, Leo,” Jessie said. “Please send him my regards and tell him I hope he gets better soon.”

“I will do, Jess,” Leo gave her a small smile. “It’s good to see you back home again.” He turned to Vicky, “And you too, Miss Donovan.”

“Leo?” Vicky’s brows knitted together as she eyed the young man who was about Jessie’s age. “Oh, my word, Leonard?” Her eyes widened.

“Guilty!” Leo held up one hand. “But please don’t call me

Leonard. That name got me picked on more than one occasion at school.

"Understood!" Vicky said. "I can relate, with my full name. Victoria!"

"That's a beautiful name," Leo told her. "But I can see how kids would twist it."

"Can I get a plate of fries with the skewered honey chicken, please?" Jess grinned. "Oh, and a cappuccino."

"Vanilla or caramel?" Leo asked Jessie.

"My usual!" Jessie told him.

"A caramel and vanilla cappuccino with whipped cream and no milk froth," Leo wrote on his pad. "What can I get for you, Miss Donovan?"

"I'll have the same as Jessie's having, including that delicious sounding coffee concoction." Vicky closed her menu and handed it to Leo. "And please also tell your dad from me that I hope he has a speedy recovery and send your mother my regards."

"I will do," Leo promised before walking off.

"What a nice guy," Vicky said. "Did you two go to school together?"

"Yes," Jessie said. "Or at least up until I skipped a few grades."

"Your mother also skipped a few grades," Vicky told her. "She was super intelligent, and you are the spitting image of her." She grinned. "You also inherited your mother's brains."

"Thank you," Jessie smiled at Vicky before going back to her father. "What are we going to do about my father and the viper?" Jessie asked suddenly.

"Jessie..." Vicky raised her eyebrows. "You know we can't interfere with that."

"Actually..." Jessie said. "After seeing that file, I think it's our duty to help him get rid of Samantha. She might be some hotshot lawyer, but she's been married three times, and each of her husbands have wound up dead."

"It says they all died of natural causes, and two of them were a lot older than she was," Vicky pointed.

"That's another red flag," Jessie said. "She only goes for men that are quite a bit older than her."

"Some women like older men," Vicky tried to reason with Jessie, who clearly thought Samantha was some sort of gold digger.

"Aunt Vicky, I really need your help with my dad," Jessie said. "We need to get Samantha out of his life before he ends up like her other three husbands."

"Jess…" Vicky sighed. "I have to admit that when I came to meet you, I was thinking along the same lines. That we need to extract your father from his current relationship."

"See," Jessie leaned forward on the table. "You're also worried about her, and as I know that you used to be in the FBI, I can only assume that you used your contacts to find out about Samantha as well."

"No," Vicky wasn't lying. She hadn't researched Samantha; she was given a file on the woman. "I didn't."

"But you're still worried enough about her that you wanted my help to convince him not to take the relationship any further?" Jessie raised an eyebrow. "Does this mean I can count on you to help me with my plan?"

"Jessie, just because she's had some bad luck with her husbands in the past doesn't mean we can judge her now," Vicky tried one more time to talk Jessie out of whatever she had up her sleeve.

"Well, then maybe this will convince you." Jessie reached into her purse and pulled out some more information on Samantha.

"What is this?" Vicky's eyes widened in shock as she read what Jessie had given her. "This can't be true."

"I'm afraid it is," Jessie said, handing Vicky the last few pages of information she had in her purse.

Vicky took all the information and put it into the folder, which she put in her purse. "I'm taking this," she told Jessie. "And if you have any copies, I'm going to need you to get them to me."

"First, tell me if you're ready to hear my plan to save my father?" Jessie told Vicky stubbornly.

"Jessie, if this information you've given me is true…" Vicky said worriedly. "Honey, I don't want you getting involved."

"Too late. The minute that woman started making a move on my father, I was involved," Jessie told Vicky. "So… are you going to help me, or must I go to Plan B, which is confronting Samantha with the copies of the information you've just taken from me."

"Fine!" Vicky relented. "But I want all the copies you have of this information, and I need you to promise me that you'll leave any interaction with Samantha to me."

"Deal!" Jessie said. "So, are you in?"

"Let's hear your plan," Vicky sighed.

"The plan came to me the other night. I remembered a story Uncle Justin told us about you and my dad when you were teenagers!" Jessie grinned as Vicky's eyes widened. "Oh, yes, we know about yours and his stolen moment in the willow grove."

Vicky felt her face flame, and her eyes widened even more. "How on earth does Justin know about that?"

"Uncle Justin was looking through his binoculars from his bedroom window when he saw you run into the willow grove looking really upset," Jessie explained. "He went to find out if you were okay as he hadn't seen my father go in after you." She looked at Vicky. "Should I continue?"

"No, it's fine," Vicky stopped the story. "Let's get to your plan, which I already know I'm not going to like."

While Vicky listened to Jessie's plan, her phone beeped with a message. Vicky glanced at the screen and froze when she saw the message was from Lee.

I'm going to ask Samantha to marry me tonight. Can you come look at the ring and let me know what you think about it?

It wasn't a few seconds after Vicky got the message when Jessie's phone rang. Jessie indicated that it was Lee. Vicky watched Jessie's expression change, and when she hung up, she did not look happy.

"That was my father," Jessie's eyes blazed. "He wants me to meet him, here of all places, in an hour because he has something important to discuss with me."

"He sent me this," Vicky said and handed Jessie her phone. "I'm sorry, Jess."

"We need to put my plan into action tonight, Aunt Vicky." Jessie handed Vicky's phone back.

Vicky sighed, closed her eyes, and pinched the bridge of her nose. Jessie was right. Vicky had thought she could listen to Jessie's plan and then tell Jessie her plan. But Lee had decided to move his marriage proposal to Samantha up, and Jessie had handed over some rather incriminating information about Samantha.

"Fine, but we do it my way," Vicky laid down the rules. "I'll get my food to go and then see if I can find out where your father is making reservations for his dinner date tonight."

Vicky waved down Leo before looking at Jessie. "Call your father back and tell him you can meet him in ten minutes instead of an hour because you have to be somewhere."

"Okay!" Jessie agreed. "Thank you, Aunt Vicky."

*L*ee walked into the corner coffee shop and saw Jessie already seated at a booth waving at him. He walked over to her and sat down.

"Hi, honey." Lee leaned over and kissed her on the cheek. "That looks good." He eyed her food.

"It is, and I can recommend it." Jessie wiped her mouth with a napkin. "Do you want me to call Leo?"

"I think he's already on his way," Lee pointed out.

Leo came to the table and took Lee's order.

"Dad, I'm glad you asked me here as I have some things I need to discuss with you," Jessie told him before he could start the conversation.

"Oh, okay!" Lee looked at Jessie, a little startled.

Jessie only ever said she wanted to discuss something with him when she'd either done something wrong or was about to drop another type of bombshell on him. Like when she was taking five months off to go on a trip around the world. Or the one he was dreading the most—I'm getting married!

Lee braced himself as he watched Jessie finish her food, sip her coffee, and then place her knife and fork neatly together on the middle of her plate. *This is bad!* Lee thought. Jessie was stalling, which meant what she was about to *discuss* with him, he was not going to like.

"Dad, so you know I told you I have this amazing job here in Key West that I'm starting next week?" Jessie looked nervously at him.

"Yes," Lee said, a frown creasing his brow. *Where is she going with this?* Lee wondered.

"Okay, so... before you freak out, I need you to stay calm and let me finish what I have to say before you comment." Jessie looked at him. "Okay?"

"Jessie, what are you trying to tell me?" Lee linked his hands together on the table.

"Dad, say you promise to let me finish before you go off the deep end?" Jessie looked at him expectantly.

"Okay," Lee unlinked his hands and held them up in a sign of surrender. "I promise."

"Pinky promise?" Jessie held out her pinky to him.

"This must be bad if you're making me make the sacred pinky promise." Lee linked his pinky finger with Jessie's. "I pinky promise."

"Great!" Jess sighed in relief and sat back against her seat. But before she could say anything, her phone that was lying face up on the table rang.

Jessie and Lee looked down at it at the same time. Jessie

immediately made a grab for the phone and tried to cover the screen.

"Sorry, Dad, I have to take this!" Jessie said, fumbling with the phone.

But the phone fell out of her hand and landed in front of him. As Lee picked the phone up to give it to Jessie, he froze when he saw the name, KW Research Labs, calling her.

"I'll take that," Jessie grabbed her phone and made a dash for the door of the cafe as she answered it.

Lee sat looking in the direction Jessie had gone, stunned at what he'd seen as it sank in what Jessie was about to tell him. The job she was starting was at Key West Research Labs. The same research lab that Georgia had worked at and Lee had been convinced had something to do with Georgia's disappearance. Jessie knew how Lee felt about the place, and that was why she'd been so secretive about her new job in Key West. Jessie had known how he'd react when he found out about it.

Lee sat staring at the door of the coffee shop, waiting for Jessie to return. His mind was reeling with thoughts of how to talk some sense into Jessie because Lee did not trust the KW Research facility, and he was surprised they'd even offered Jessie a job because they must know who her mother was. Then another horrible thought struck Lee. What if they had hired Jessie because of who her mother was?

"Sorry, Dad," Jessie said when she came back to the table and put her phone down as she slid into the booth.

"Jessie, was what you wanted to tell me that your new job was at KW Research Labs?" Lee asked her as calmly as he possibly could.

"Oh, shoot!" Jessie said. "I'd hoped you hadn't seen that." She reached over and placed her hand over his. "I know how you feel about the company, but it was never proven that the facility had anything to do with Mom's disappearance. If anything, they were trying to help Mom with her investigation."

"Jessie, you're an adult now, and I can't tell you what to do," Lee sighed. "But, honey, promise me you'll be vigilant and only do what your job requires you to do. Don't get into anything that could get you into trouble."

"Dad, you know how cautious I am," Jessie assured him. "But I do feel relieved that you now know. It's been eating me alive since I accepted the job, and I just didn't know how to tell you."

"My feelings about KW Research Facility aside, I know it's a hard place to get into, so a big part of me is very proud of you," Lee gave Jessie's hand that was covering his a loving squeeze.

Jessie was about to say something when her phone rang once again. This time it was from someone named Oli K. "So sorry, Dad," Jessie picked up her phone. "But I have to take this call."

Jessie answered her phone, only this time she didn't leave the table, and while she spoke on her phone, Lee's food arrived. He'd only ordered a sandwich because he had another stop to make after this before he went back to the office. Jessie didn't speak on the phone long.

"I'm so sorry, Dad, but I have to go," Jessie told him, gathering up her things in readiness to leave. "Thank you so much for meeting me and for being so understanding about my new job."

"Of course, honey," Lee said as he watched her stand up, lean over, and kiss his cheek.

"Enjoy your lunch, and I'm so sorry I can't stay, but KW wants me to be there in thirty minutes, and I need to go home and change quickly," Jessie smiled down at him. "Can we chat tonight about what you wanted to tell me? Although I think I know what it is. You've decided to take Uncle Shaun up on his offer to take over Donovan Law."

"Well..." Lee was once again interrupted by the sound of Jessie's phone.

"I'll see you later, Dad," Jessie didn't give him a chance to say another word before she dashed out of the coffee shop, leaving Lee once again sitting stunned as he watched her go.

"Can I get you anything else, Mr. Young?" Leo came over to his table to ask.

"Could you perhaps make this to go?" Lee handed Leo his plate. "It seems my lunch date had another appointment."

"No problem," Leo took the plate. "I'll be right back."

While Leo went to wrap up Lee's sandwich to go, he took out his phone and called Vicky.

"Hello?" Vicky answered.

"Hi, it seems my daughter had to rush off, and I find myself free," Lee told her. "Any chance that I can stop by in, say, ten minutes instead of an hour?"

"Sure," Vicky said. "I'm at the dance studio the entire day today."

Lee hung up, took his wrapped lunch from Leo, paid the bill, and left to go meet Vicky. He was once again glad that Vicky was back in town as he'd always found her easy to talk to, and right now, he needed that.

Chapter Six

THE LADDER INCIDENT

Cory called Vicky to the front desk to let her know that Lee was there to see her. Vicky told Cory to send Lee through to studio three, where she was measuring blinds. Vicky was reaching over as far as she could with her tape measure when Lee walked into the room and startled her. Her ladder wobbled and dislodged her, and she felt herself being thrown from the ladder.

Vicky was sure she was about to land on the springboard floor, but before she hit it, a pair of warm, strong arms caught her.

"Careful!" Lee breathed, looking down at her cradled in his arms.

Vicky could see the panic in his eyes and feel his rapid heartbeat with her ear pressing up against his solid chest.

"Thank you for catching me," Vicky said breathlessly.

"You should know better than to lean so far over when you are on a rickety old ladder," Lee said, still holding her and making no move to put her down.

"It's not a rickety old ladder," Vicky said. "You can put me down now."

"Oh..." Lee looked down at her, his cheeks reddened slightly. "Of course." He gently lowered her to her feet. "But, Vicky, you have to be more careful. If I wasn't here...." His face paled, and he shook his head.

"I know," Vicky smiled at him, touching his arm. "I promise to be more careful going forward."

"Good!" Lee sighed in relief. "Would you like some help measuring while I'm here?"

"Yes, that would be awesome," Vicky accepted his offer. "Here, you take the book and write down the measurements." She shoved the book and pen towards him.

"No," Lee didn't take the items. He took his jacket off, placed it on the piano, and loosened his tie. "You write down the measurements, and I'll take them."

"You know if you fall off the ladder, I can't catch you?" Vicky pointed out.

"But you're here to call an ambulance if I do fall!" Lee told her with a grin.

"Marvelous!" Vicky pulled a face.

Lee and Vicky chatted as they worked. Lee began by telling Vicky about his meeting with Jessie.

"I think you handled that well," Vicky said honestly. "You were right to say that she's an adult now and that you have to respect her decision. I agree with you that being invited to join KW Research facility is indeed something to be proud of."

"Yes, but that still doesn't mean I trust Jessie working there." Lee measured the last of the windows and gave Vicky the measurement. "I'm going to be worried about her every day she goes into work."

"But wouldn't you do that no matter where she worked?" Vicky pointed out.

"Yes, but at least at another company, I wouldn't have what happened to Georgia constantly on my mind." Lee climbed off the ladder.

"There was nothing at KW Research pointing to them having anything to do with Georgia's disappearance," Vicky reminded Lee.

"That's exactly what Jessie said before someone named Oli K called her." Lee picked up the ladder. "Where do you want this?"

"I have to measure the windows in the ballroom dancing studio," Vicky said absently, her brow furrowing. "Did you say Oli K?"

"Yes," Lee said, looking at Vicky curiously. "Why? Do you know who Oli K is?"

"I might!" Vicky told him. "But I'm not sure how Jessie would know the Oli K I know."

"She could," Lee pointed out. "Maybe they met at the university?"

"You could be right. I think the person I'm thinking of also went to Harvard," Vicky told Lee. "I'll ask Jessie tonight. She asked me to dinner."

"Oh?" Lee looked a little surprised. "She didn't tell me that."

"Maybe it slipped her mind," Vicky said with a warm smile. "What did Jessie say when you told her about your pending engagement?"

Vicky led them to the ballroom studio while Lee carried the ladder behind her. Lee stopped at the entrance to the room and looked around.

"Wow, it's been a long time since I was in this room!" Lee smiled and walked into the room, looking around as he positioned the ladder where Vicky pointed for it to be placed.

"Are you avoiding my question?" Vicky looked at him suspiciously.

"No," Lee shook his head. "I didn't get a chance to tell her."

"Ah…" Vicky nodded. "So, are you going to go ahead with the proposal tonight?"

"No," Lee shook his head. "I don't want to do anything behind Jessie's back, and this affects her as well."

"But she's a grown woman now…." Vicky shook her head and sighed. "Isn't it time you lived your life for you now?"

"You know, Christy said something along those same lines." Lee climbed up the ladder. "When I was thinking about asking

Samantha out and telling Christy that I'd met someone, but I wanted to tell Jessie first."

"Lee..." Vicky jotted down the measurements Lee gave her. "Why are you suddenly in such a hurry to ask Samantha to marry you?"

"I wasn't," Lee let the current blind down and measured it. "But I heard through a colleague that Samantha was offered a job in Seattle and was thinking about taking it."

"Seattle?" Vicky's brows shot up.

"Yes, her mother is from Seattle," Lee said, winding the blind back up. "Whoever built these windows didn't do a very good job. They are all slightly different in size."

"Mrs. Amelia warned me about the windows," Vicky told Lee. "Her grandfather built this building, and as he didn't have a fortune to spend on supplies, he had to take what he could get. But he did try to get them as close to size as he could."

"Did Mrs. Amelia ever think about redoing them?" Lee asked as he moved along to the next window.

"No, and why would she?" Vicky looked at him. "It was built by her grandfather, and the windows lend character to the property."

"I guess that's one way of looking at it," Lee told her the measurements.

"Getting back to your impending engagement." Vicky steered the conversation back to Lee's relationship with Samantha. "What are you going to do?"

"I guess just go to dinner with Samantha tonight and wait until I can have a conversation with my daughter without her phone nearby." Lee once again climbed down the ladder. "Is that it?"

"Yes, thank you." Vicky grinned. "You can leave the ladder. I'll get Dante to put it away in the shed out the back."

"Okay," Lee dusted off his hands and looked around the room again. "Wasn't there a trophy case in here?"

"Are you looking for all your trophies?" Vicky laughed and shook her head. "One of the things Mrs. Amelia insisted on taking with her was the trophy case and all her favorite students' pictures."

"Where on earth is she going to put all those items in her small house at the retirement village?" Lee asked, amazed.

"In her garage," Vicky told him. Her eyes landed on the mini sound system sitting on a small table at the far side of the room. "When was the last time you danced?" she asked, making her way towards the system.

"Not since I hung my dance shoes up and hightailed it out of Key West to go to university," Lee admitted.

Vicky grinned, took out her phone, scrolled to find a track, and linked her phone to the sound system. A foxtrot sounded through the speakers positioned throughout the room, and Vicky held out her hand to Lee challengingly.

"Let's see if you remember any of those championship moves!" Vicky grinned.

"Seriously?" Lee asked her with a cringing look on his face. "I'll probably break a few of your toes."

"Oh, come on, it's like riding a bike," Vicky coaxed him.

"Fine, but just one dance!" Lee loosened his tie more and rolled up his sleeves. "I can't believe I'm doing this," he muttered, taking Vicky's hand and pulling her to him. "Don't say I didn't warn you when you end up with a few toe casts."

"I'll take my chances," Vicky laughed and relaxed into his strong arms when Lee took charge and led them expertly around the floor.

They got so swept up in the music and enjoying dancing with each other again that one dance led into another. They were coming to the end of their fourth dance when applause coming from the door startled them, and they turned to see Christy, Justin, and Ty cheering them on.

"Way to go, big brother!" Justin whistled. "I'd forgotten how good you and Vicky were together ballroom dancing."

"Thank you," Lee said, breathing a little heavily from the exercise.

"A little out of shape there, old man!" Ty laughed at his cousin.

Vicky turned off the music and greeted her visitors. "Have you all come to sign up for lessons?"

"After seeing how much fun that was," Justin said. "I may just do that."

"You're just thinking of meeting single women," Ty threw at Justin.

"I guess that would be one of the perks!" Justin grinned. "But, to be honest, I've missed dancing. It was always time we spent with Mom when she'd help us practice."

"Actually, I mentioned I was going to stop by the studio on my way home to take a look around, and these two were in my office and decided to come with me," Christy explained to Vicky. "I must say I'm so glad you've decided to add ballroom and ballet again. It was so sad when Mrs. Amelia stopped them and concentrated on modern dance."

"Jessie took ballet," Lee told Vicky. "She loved Mrs. Amelia."

"So did Hannah," Christy said. "Mya, on the other hand." She rolled her eyes. "She hated any type of dancing. She preferred swimming and gymnastics."

"But gymnasts can make great dancers," Vicky said. "We were both gymnasts."

"I did tell her that, but she went to three lessons and decided she still hated dancing, and that was that," Christy shrugged.

"That was such a pity because Mya is so elegant and graceful," Vicky sighed. "Can I get any of you some tea, coffee, water?"

"Not for us," Justin said, including Ty when he declined Vicky's offer. "We have to go meet with the psychologist who is evaluating Roberta Davies."

"She's the arsonist!" Vicky looked at Justin.

"That's right." Justin nodded.

"I'm sorry I wasn't here when all that was going on," Vicky looked at Christy.

"Hey, I'm just glad you're here at all," Christy assured Vicky. "And even happier that you're staying for good."

"Well, we'd better be off," Ty patted Justin on the shoulder. "I hope you're going to have a grand opening ball, Vicky."

"That's not a bad idea," Vicky said.

"Sounds good to me!" Justin agreed.

"If you're serious, I would love to help you plan that," Christy told Vicky.

"Hey, back off Vicky, she's only just got here and has a lot of work to do in the studio," Lee admonished his siblings.

"It was just an idea!" Ty shook his head as he looked at his cousin.

Vicky could see there was still a bit of tension between Lee and Ty. She had felt it the other night when she'd arrived at their house for dinner. Vicky would've thought that after all these years, they would've worked it out and finally gotten over their stupid falling out. When the Young family had thought that Aaron had jilted Shannon, Christy's twin sister, and worse left her alone and pregnant, the only one that had stood up for Aaron had been Ty.

That hadn't gone well with Lee, and he and Ty had had a huge falling out, which had only got even worse throughout their university years because Ty was still good friends with Aaron. Ty had even tried to get Christy to go with him to Miami the year before Ty joined the FBI, but Lee had stepped in and forbade it. As Christy was still not over the shock of Shannon's death, she'd sided with Lee, saying she wasn't ready to see the man she blamed for Shannon's death.

That episode had widened the rift between Ty and Lee. Ty had gone off to Virginia and then traveled around a lot once he'd graduated from FBI training. He had barely come home except for Christmas or his aunt's or uncle's birthdays. Over the years, Lee and Ty had slowly become more civil to each other until Lee's mother died. After that, they had come together in their shock and grief after Aunt Lucy's death. After Ty was shot and almost died two years ago, he and Lee had gotten closer once again.

Ty had only been back in Key West for about seven weeks

when his uncle Jake, Lee's father, died suddenly of a heart attack. Ty hadn't fully recovered himself when Jake had died, and as he'd insisted on participating in the funeral, he somehow managed to get an infection in his wound. Ty had nearly died of blood poisoning four days after Jake's funeral, and it had been Lee who'd found Ty passed out on his bathroom floor. It had been Lee that had refused to leave Ty's bedside at the hospital until he was sure Ty was going to pull through.

Christy had told Vicky that after Ty nearly died, he and Lee's relationship had gotten a lot better, although Christy wasn't convinced it was as strong as it once was. Vicky watched Lee talking to Ty and Justin about Roberta Davies before Ty and Justin said their goodbyes and left.

"I need to get going as well," Lee walked towards Vicky and Christy, rolling down his shirt sleeves and fixing his tie. "I'll get my jacket and be on my way."

"Thanks for the help," Vicky said as Lee said goodbye and turned to leave. "Would you like to dance with me?" she grinned at Christy.

"Heavens, no," Christy shook her head. "I think Mya's disdain for dance has rubbed off on me."

"Never!" Vicky shook her head and put her arms around her best friend's shoulder, leading her from the room. "I know that deep down, you still love to dance." Vicky walked into her office. "So, how about some coffee or tea?"

"I'd love a cup of peppermint tea, please," Christy said, taking off her hat and sitting down. "It's been a long day."

"That's right, you have new recruits," Vicky messaged Cory for some peppermint tea.

"It's not only that," Christy told Vicky. "Battalion Chief Patricia Kingcaid, whom I'm standing in for, may not be coming back. So, I spent the day being bombarded with calls from the fire chief. He wants me to take over the position permanently."

"Christy, that's wonderful!" Vicky breathed.

"I guess!" Christy shrugged.

"Uh, oh," Vicky sat back in her chair. "I know that look. What's up?"

"After what happened with Roberta and finding out everything I have recently about Shannon, Aaron, and even the shock about Dustin having kept such a huge secret from me," Christy sighed. "I feel out of sorts."

"Are you saying you no longer want to work for the fire department?" Vicky's brows drew together. "Christy, that's all you ever talked about when we were discussing our careers."

"Well, look at you..." Christy pointed out. "You had an exciting career. You were a freakin' CIA agent, for goodness' sake." She lowered her voice. "Then you joined the FBI."

"And now I own a dance studio!" Vicky made a show with her hands. "I see your point."

"Do you?" Christy asked, confusion shining in her eyes. "Because if you do, could you explain it to me?" She flopped back in the chair and clasped her hands in front of her. "All I wanted was to move up the ranks and get as far as I could go until I retired from the fire department." She looked down at her hands, fiddling with her thumbs. "But now that I'm up for this new promotion...." When she looked up at Vicky, her eyes were shadowed. "I don't feel as excited about it as I should be."

"Christy, you just went through a harrowing experience," Vicky leaned forward on her desk. "You were kidnapped and tied to a chair by an arsonist who thought she was cleansing the earth of evil, for goodness' sake. You're bound to be having doubts about your choice of career if not a bit of PTSD."

"You're probably right," Christy sighed. "I'm still getting over the shock of everything that happened recently."

"Why don't you take some time off, go on a vacation, or stay here with me and we'll do some of those crazy adrenaline-fueled extreme sports challenges we used to like to do," Vicky offered.

"That sounds wonderful," Christy admitted. "And I do have a lot of accumulated leave."

"There you go," Vicky smiled. "That's settled then. Get the

promotion, put in for leave, and we'll find some action-packed crazy sports challenges to do."

"Not too crazy, though," Christy surprised Vicky by saying. "We're not as young as we were, and we have to be a little more careful with our health."

"Who are you, and what have you done with my friend Christy?" Vicky pulled a funny face. "Wasn't that me who used to say things like that when you showed me the crazy stuff you'd signed us up for?"

"Yes, that was you," Christy laughed. "But back then, falling and breaking a hip was nothing compared to what falling and breaking a hip at our age would do."

"Says the one that hasn't even turned fifty yet," Vicky teased. "Speaking of your fiftieth...."

"Please don't!" Christy held up her hand. "I've said a million times I don't want a big surprise party, and before you deny it, remember I'm a mom to three kids and a niece. I have eyes in the back of my head, and I *know* everything that goes on around me."

"Well, then this is going to come as a surprise to you," Vicky assured Christy. "Because we're not planning anything, and the family was going to surprise you by honoring your wishes of keeping your birthday low-key."

"Of course, you all were!" Christy rolled her eyes in disbelief. "Changing the subject." She looked at Vicky, "I hear you're going to meet Jessie's new boyfriend tonight."

"Am I?" Vicky's brows knitted together. She was genuinely surprised to hear that. "I know Jessie and I are having dinner tonight...." She stopped and looked at Christy. "You should join us."

"That's sweet," Christy smiled. "But I have plans with Aaron tonight, and we've already met the new man in Jessie's life. His name's Oliver. They met at Harvard, and I believe they are both starting work at KW Research Facility."

"Would Oliver's last name happen to be Kelly?" Vicky asked Christy

"Yes, how did you know that?" Christy looked at Vicky curiously.

"I know Oliver's mother. She's my new ballet teacher. They've moved into the Shaw house," Vicky explained to Christy. "And Lee told me when he and Jessie were having lunch earlier that she got a call from someone named Oli K before ditching him and rushing off."

"Does Lee know about KW Research yet?" Christy asked and stopped talking when Cory walked into the room with two steaming cups of peppermint tea. She thanked the young woman, who smiled and left the room.

"Yes, Jessie told him at lunch today before she went rushing off, presumably to meet Oliver," Vicky put some honey in her tea and stirred it. "What makes you think Jessie is going to introduce me to Oliver tonight?"

So that is who Jessie was going to bring as the plus one she said she was bringing, Vicky thought. Vicky hoped that Oliver wasn't where she'd gotten the information about Samantha from because that would mean he'd used Robin's access to get the information. That would not be good for Robin, Oliver, or Jessie.

"She told me this afternoon," Christy put some brown sugar into her tea. "We met him last night."

"Why did she introduce him to you and now me before introducing him to her father?" Vicky took a cautious sip of her brew.

"I think she's looking for us to vet him before introducing him to Lee," Christy said.

"We can't blame her, really," Vicky said. "Lee was a nightmare when we started dating. I can only imagine what he's like with his daughter. Especially as Lee has been both father and mother to her since Jessie was two."

"Yes, he can be a bit of a bear about the guys Jessie dates." Christy shook her head. "But don't worry, he is just as picky with Mya." She laughed. "He even picks the girls Luke dates to bits and has been trying to get Luke to ask one of my lieutenant's daughters out for months now."

"Do you mean Dr. Tara Bright, the beautiful surgeon?" Vicky grinned. "I saw the way Luke looked at her the other night at the family dinner."

"She looks at him the same way, but as far as we all know, neither of them has had the courage to ask each other out," Christy shook her head in exasperation.

"Maybe we should do it for them," Vicky suggested.

"Vicky, I know that look!" Christy raised her eyebrows. "I don't think we should meddle in Luke's love life."

"We won't meddle," Vicky said innocently. "We'll simply gently nudge them together."

"You are such a romantic," Christy grinned. "What about you?" She looked at Vicky questioningly. "When are you going to get back into the dating scene?"

"I'm nowhere close to being ready!" Vicky held up her hands. "Speaking of going out, I have to go get ready for my dinner with Jessie soon."

"Yes, and I should get going as I'm going out with Aaron," Christy finished her tea.

"I'll walk with you to the parking lot," Vicky said, getting her purse and closing her office door as they left. "Cory, I'm going for the day. Please lock up."

Cory promised to lock up before they said their goodbyes and left.

"Don't be too hard on Jessie about not letting you know about Oliver," Christy said, climbing into her SUV.

"I'll try not to," Vicky promised.

Christy said goodbye, started her car, and left. Vicky stood watching Christy leave before she climbed into her car. The moment she sat in her seat, the hair at the back of her neck prickled. Her hand slid into her purse, but before she reached for her weapon, a familiar deep voice warned her not to move a muscle.

"What are you doing here?" Vicky hissed, not turning around.

"This is not the place for this conversation," his voice was low and dangerous. "Drive."

Vicky started her car, and as she backed out of the parking lot, she noticed some bags on the floor of the passenger side.

"I see you've figured out where we're going!" he said as Vicky pulled into the road and headed away from the direction she'd normally go to go home.

Chapter Seven

JESSIE'S SECRET BOYFRIEND

"Are you going to tell me why you decided to break into my car and get me to give you a ride?" Vicky asked him. Her voice held no hint of fear. Instead, it was laced with anger.

"I came to find out when you're going to free me?" he said in a low, gruff, impatient voice.

"Can you please just be a little more patient?" Vicky shook her head in exasperation. "As you know, I'm working on getting the evidence I need."

"Well, work faster," he growled. "I can't take the cramped living space or the constant pacing. I don't think that guy you've forced me to bunk with ever sleeps!"

"Will you stop whining?!" Vicky glanced in the mirror at the man.

He was ruggedly handsome with sandy brown hair and blue-green eyes. The scar that ran close to the side of his left eye and all the way down to his neck didn't distract from his looks, and it made him look tough. But right now, you couldn't see the scar on his cheek and neck as he looked like he hadn't shaved in at least four or five days.

"Are you growing a beard?" Vicky moved her mirror to look at him.

"So what if I am growing a beard?" he grumbled. "I hardly get any time in the bathroom to shave with my new roommate!" he hissed. "Seriously, if you don't do something soon, I won't be held responsible for my actions." He glanced back in the mirror. "Shouldn't you be keeping your eyes on the road and not me?"

"Just a few more days," Vicky sighed. "Now, what is this really about? All this cloak and dagger? Because I don't think you came to see me just to scare me half to death."

"I have that information for you that you asked me to look into this afternoon." The man slid a file on the passenger seat. "I hope this information helps you speed things up so you can get back to freeing me!"

Vicky pulled into a parking space. It was an old mini mall that had closed down years ago and then abandoned. She opened the file on her passenger seat. Her eyes widened as she sifted through the information she found in it.

"This is the original file?" Vicky looked up at the man in her rearview mirror.

"Yes," he nodded.

"There must've been a mixup," Vicky said, not wanting to believe what he was implying. "The file could've been switched at the agency."

"It could've." He raised his eyebrows, staring back at her in the mirror. "But then there's this." He leaned over and handed her an envelope with a few photos in it. "The first one was taken two hours ago." He flopped back against the back seat. "You need to be more careful who you let into your inner circle, V."

"There could be many explanations for this," Vicky stared at the photo in her hand. Tiny tingles of shock vibrated through her fingertips, making her hand shake slightly. "Why do you automatically think the worst of people?"

"Because you and I both know that even the most perfect looking apple can be completely rotten on the inside," he said, taking an apple from his pocket. "To make matters worse, this is who your target really is." He handed her another file.

When Vicky opened it, she couldn't believe her eyes. It

wasn't possible because Vicky knew firsthand that the person staring back at her was dead because Vicky was there when the person died.

"This doesn't make any sense," Vicky looked up into her mirror at him. "Are you sure it's the same person?" She looked at one of the other photos in the envelope of the person in question. "I can see a slight resemblance."

"I've never been surer of anything in my life," he absently rubbed the section of the scar near his eye. "I would know that face anywhere. No matter how many times one tries to change it, you can never change your eyes or what's in your soul." His eyes were cold when they stared back in the mirror. "And don't forget I more than anyone knows what's in that particular person's soul!"

"What is their end game?" Vicky bit her lip. "Is the agency involved because I don't believe for one minute anyone in my team would betray me." She shook her head. "And if the agency is aware of this, why feed me false information? Why even put me on this mission? What could they possibly accomplish by sending me on a wild goose chase?"

"I could think of a few reasons!" He pulled an apple out of his pocket. "Oh, you're out of apples at home."

"You were in my house again?" Vicky's eyes flew to meet his eyes in the mirror before something dawned on her, and she looked at the newest photo he'd given her. "That's where you took this from...." She glared at him in the mirror. "You were in my room?"

"It had the best view for me to get that shot." He shrugged unapologetically.

"Unbelievable!" Vicky shook her head. "You're so lucky that I need your help as much as you need mine," she hissed.

"Oh, come on." He grinned. "You know it's much more than that, cousin!"

"You know you have to keep quiet about us being related. We can't let anyone know, not even your roommate, that we know we are related," Vicky warned him. "That would lead them straight to our sideline investigation. If anyone knew we were looking into that doctor and his connection to KW Labs...."

"I know!" the man assured her. "Although that would have been one of my guesses as to why the agency has sent you on a wild goose chase with your current mission."

"You think they somehow know?" Vicky's eyes widened.

"Not only that, I think they are trying to find the treasure trove you're hiding," he told her. "That would make sense as to why they put you on the trail of not just any black widow, but *the* black widow."

"If what you're saying is true..." Vicky looked at him, concerned. "Then that means...."

"You can't trust anyone in your inner circle or your safety net at the agency," he pointed out. "Welcome to my side."

"I can't believe that," Vicky swallowed, her throat suddenly feeling dry. "I've worked with my team, except three of them, for years. They've always had my back."

"Have any of them been asking subtle questions about any item in your treasure trove?" He took another bite of his apple. "Especially the one who was passing something to the target less than a few hours ago."

"No," Vicky told him honestly. "But I'm going to keep a closer eye on all of them."

"Including your lawyer's daughter?" He took another bite of his apple.

"She has nothing to do with this," Vicky told him defensively. "Leave her out of this. She's working at KW Labs."

"And you don't find it all suspicious how she got that information she gave you earlier today?" he asked her. "Or how she wants you to help her with her plan to break up her father and his girlfriend?"

"How could you know about that, unless...." Her eyes narrowed as she glared up at him. "Are you spying on me?"

"I'm not spying on you, V," his voice dropped. "I'm keeping you safe. I owe you my life, and you know I take that seriously.

You could've left me or just believed what everyone else did. But you didn't."

"You would've done the same for me, or at least I like to think so." Vicky bit her lip as her mind worried over the implications of the information he'd just given her. "We'd better get moving. I have to meet Jessie Young for dinner and meet her boyfriend."

She picked up her phone and sent a quick message to Jessie.

> *Running a few minutes late, can we meet at your house?*

"That's something else that is far too coincidental for my liking," he told her. "What are the odds of Jessie Young meeting Oliver Kelly? The son of one of your team members, who also happens to be going to work for KW Research Labs?"

"As they both went to Harvard around the same time and studied the same thing..." Jessie said. "I think the chances of them meeting were pretty good."

Vicky put her phone into her bag before starting the car and pulling it back onto the road they'd been traveling on.

"Before we accuse anyone of anything, I need more information," Vicky caught his eyes in the mirror. "You more than anyone should know what it feels like to be convicted on mere perception."

"Touché!" he said.

"You know if the target really is who you say they are, then it changes everything about my case," Vicky told him. "It also gives me a whole new layer to my investigation because now I have to figure out if the person who assigned me this case gave me misinformation or if the files were switched somewhere between."

"Another one of my theories on that is that the agency really doesn't know who the target is," he said, finishing off his apple. "But looking into the person because they've stolen someone's identity, who was also on the FBI person of interest list."

"But you are doubtful that's the case," Vicky said.

"You never know, though. Some people don't tend to stay dead in our line of work!" he said. "We know our fair share of people who are thought dead." He grinned.

"But what are the chances that a target popped up on the agency's radar with a stolen identity without them figuring it out?" Vicky shook her head.

"Yes, that's what drew me to the conclusion that neither of the previous theories are correct." He leaned forward. "V, I think you're in danger."

"If I am, that means it trickles down to a lot of others." Vicky's pulse started to race as her mind turned. "How quickly can you get ready to move?"

"You do know that I'll only move if you're coming with me," he made it clear to her.

"You don't have to worry about me," Vicky tried to assure him. "I need to know that you can get ready to move on short notice."

"Of course," he said. "But V, I'm being serious. This time I think you're in too deep, and if my number one theory is right about what's going on, you spooking the nest to get all your chicks to fly away is exactly what whoever's behind this wants."

"Only you're the one that will be moving my treasure trove while I play along, seemingly oblivious to knowing what I do now," Vicky's eyes narrowed as her mind settled on the best play forward. "There are a few things I need you to do for me because I have a plan. A risky one, but if your theory is true, then I've been herded here for more reasons than just finding my treasure trove. I need you to find out where Roberta Davies is being kept."

"The arsonist?" His brows furrowed thoughtfully. "Why do you need to know her whereabouts?"

"I think that either the agency or some other law enforcement has reopened a cold case," Vicky swore under her breath. "One that could collide with our own investigation into KW Labs."

"Okay, let me see what I can find," he promised her. "Do you want me to get the information on those recent house fires?"

"Yes," Vicky nodded. "When you find Roberta Davies, figure out how I can get in to talk to her." She glanced at him in her mirror. "I think she's been holding back information."

"You can drop me at the end of the next street," he instructed. "Remember, you can't go gung ho and face down anyone in your inner circle about this new information. You have to continue as if you're investigating the original case."

"Of course not," Vicky pulled into the road and turned towards the bank of trees. "Now, I need you to get rid of all the bugs or other devices you've planted on or around me."

"Nope," he shook his head as he waited for Vicky to open her car door and hop out. "V, there's a deadly assassin who I think is gunning for you. I also know all about your idiotic plan to poke that particular deadly creature. So, no! They stay where they are."

"Fine, but you have to promise me that you'll get out if you have to on my orders!" She slid out of the car, taking a sack of recyclables he'd given her to the recycling bins that lined the street curb. "You know you really should do your own recycling and not make me do it for you."

"That way, they think it's yours!" He grinned at her. "While you're recycling, will you put this in the compost bin?" He handed her his apple core, saying softly, "There are still a lot of apples with perfect cores."

Before Vicky could answer, he'd slipped out the driver's door and disappeared into the thicket of trees. Vicky gave a short laugh and shook her head.

Once Vicky had put the recycling the man had left on her passenger side floor into the bin, she slid back into her car and headed home. She didn't have a lot of time left to get ready. Vicky glanced at her passenger seat and noted that the information he'd shown her was gone, and she smiled. The man had always been thorough and was one of the only people she knew she could trust. And if his theory was right, she was glad he was on her side.

*V*icky, Jessie, and Oliver arrived at the restaurant and were seated at their table. Vicky had kept her questions to herself when Jessie asked her if they could pick up Oliver, as his rental car hadn't been delivered. Vicky thought she'd rather wait until Jessie and Oliver were together to ask questions about their relationship. That way, she would be better able to read them.

Vicky sat patiently while the waiter gave them their menus and took their beverage orders.

"I can tell by how quiet you've been that you are waiting for the right time to ask us questions, Aunt Vicky," Jessie leaned forward on the table. "So let me start by answering what I assume are at least three of them."

"First, I do know that you and Oliver's mother, Robin, work together," Jessie told Vicky. "Oliver and I met at Harvard. We had a genetics, microbiology, and biochemistry class together."

"You have the same look on your face my mother had yesterday when I finally introduced her to my girlfriend of four years," Oliver told Vicky.

"I thought I was being rather neutral," Vicky raised an eyebrow.

"Exactly!" Oliver made a rotation with his index finger. "My mother also gets what I call her wooden plank look when she's secretly scrutinizing and interrogating me."

"Did you say that the two of you have been dating for four years?" Vicky's eyes narrowed. She looked at Jessie. "How come you've never introduced each other to your parents before now?"

"We started off as friends for the first two years at university," Jessie told Vicky. "As for keeping it from my father, you know how overprotective he is. He was also living over a thousand miles away from me while I was in Boston," Jessie pointed out.

"I knew that if he knew I was dating anyone, it would only increase his worry, especially after my first attempt at dating in my final year of high school."

"Fair enough," Vicky leaned back with her hands on the table as she watched Jessie. Jessie's first boyfriend was in the same year as her and had become obsessed with Jessie. It was a situation that had ended badly, leaving Jessie traumatized and Lee becoming even more protective of her. "But how do you think he's going to feel now when he meets your boyfriend of four years?"

"Aunt Vicky, I wanted to tell him," Jessie admitted. "But Uncle Justin and Uncle Ty told me it was better not to. Dad had just stopped his obsession with my mother's case and was finally moving into a good place when Oliver and I started dating."

"Ty and Justin know about the two of you?" Vicky's eyes widened.

"Yes, they have since the first year Oli and I started officially dating," Jessie replied to Vicky's question.

"I wouldn't mention that to your dad!" Vicky advised her before turning to Oliver. "And what about your mother? How do you think she's going to feel about you keeping your relationship a secret all these years?"

"As you know, Aunt Vicky." Oliver put his hand over Jessie's on the table. "My mother had just lost my father the year before Jessie and I got together. She was not in a good place." Vicky watched Oliver's eyes become shadowed when he mentioned his father. "After what happened to my father, I'm sure you remember how paranoid Mom got."

"Oliver didn't want his mother putting me under a microscope or thinking the exact same thing that we know you're thinking right now." Jessie looked at Vicky pointedly.

"And what would that be?" Vicky asked Jessie.

"That Oliver and I meeting and falling in love is way too coincidental and convenient!" Jessie guessed accurately. "Because of the line of work you're in, your mind is already ticking over and has made a mental note to check our story at the first opportunity you get."

"Jessie told me that she was sure her father saw me call her this afternoon while she was at lunch and that her father probably already told you," Oliver said before Vicky could say anything. "Or that Christy, who we had dinner with last night, might have said something."

"So, Oliver and I know that both you and his mother have already started looking into our relationship," Jessie once again guessed accurately. "And you're both wondering if we've been recruited by some agency. So, we'll put your mind at rest and tell you that Oliver and I applied to KW Research labs together."

"Jessie and I are serious about each other." Oliver looked at Jessie and smiled when she looked back at him. It was then that Vicky saw that they really did love each other. "I knew my mom wanted to retire and teach ballet. She always wanted to live in Florida."

"I wanted to move back to Key West to be closer to my family." Jessie put her hand on Oliver's. "So, we both applied to KW Research Labs because they do have one of the most advanced labs in the country for scientists in our field of work."

"But we knew the chances of us both getting in were slim," Oliver continued. "So, we both also applied to three other labs that were within commuting distance to Key West."

"It was very fortunate that you were both accepted for the program at Key West Research Labs," Vicky said. "Why wouldn't they take you both? You are both brilliant, excelled in your fields." She opened the bottle of water that the waiter had put next to each of their place settings when they were seated. "Your father, Oliver, was also a brilliant scientist, as was Jessie's mother. So, you both also have a great scientific pedigree."

"We were also both offered the research programs at the other three research labs we applied for." Jessie picked up her purse and pulled out a file that she handed to Vicky.

"Are there any more files in that bag of yours, Mary

Poppins?" Vicky glanced down at Jessie's square purse, taking the file from Jessie and examining the contents.

"No," Jessie shook her head.

"This is impressive," Vicky said to both of them. "But, do you mind if I keep this?"

"Yes, that's your copy," Jessie surprised Vicky by saying.

"My mother has one too," Oliver told Vicky.

Vicky put the file down on the empty chair beside her, beneath her purse and coat. She sat back in her chair and looked at the couple sitting in front of her. Their body language spoke volumes to Vicky. To the untrained eye, Jessie and Oliver might have seemed as cool as cucumbers, but Vicky could see how nervous they were. While there was no doubting how they felt about each other, there was still something they were not telling her.

"We were also above board about our relationship with KW Research Labs when we came to Key West fourteen months ago for our first interviews," Jessie told Vicky. "They said that they had no policy against their employees dating. But we would have to fill in the correct paperwork."

"Which we both did on the day of the initial interview," Oliver assured Vicky.

"Wait!" Vicky stopped Jessie and Oliver. "You came here for an interview over a year ago?"

"Yes." Jessie and Oliver said together.

"Why do you ask, Aunt Vicky?" Oliver's eyes narrowed.

"What day exactly?" Vicky asked.

"It was November sixth of last year," Jessie told Vicky. "It was a Friday. Oliver and I came to Key West for the weekend."

"I stayed in a hotel," Oliver explained. "That was the weekend Jessie showed me the Shaw house and told me that the owners were thinking of renting it out."

"So, this is why you told me about the Shaw house being up for rent when you knew I was moving back to Key West and looking for a place for my new ballet instructor and her son?" Vicky looked at Jessie accusingly.

"Yes, guilty!" Jessie admitted with a sly smile.

"You two should've been in the CIA!" Vicky told them. Although she was still convinced they were not telling her everything, she was impressed at how they'd managed to keep their relationship a secret for four years.

"Jessie knew that Mrs. Amelia wanted to retire and sell her dance studio," Oliver told Vicky. "The weekend we were both here for the interview, we went to see Mrs. Amelia. Jessie knew you were in the process of selling your house and dance studio in Miami to move back to Key West."

"That explains why Mrs. Amelia called me out of the blue to offer me her dance studio." Vicky shook her head in amazement. "I was so busy getting my life back together that I didn't even stop to think about her timing."

"Oli and I just wanted you, my father, and his mother to be happy," Jessie explained. "We wanted to live in the same town and have our parents close by."

"So, you two manipulated Robin and me?" Vicky looked impressed.

"We did, and we won't apologize for it," Jessie told her flatly. "You are looking a lot more relaxed than you ever did when I visited you in Miami over these past two years, Aunt Vicky."

"I am happy to be home and was even more thrilled to get Mrs. Amelia's dance studio," Vicky admitted. "But it's not a nice feeling to feel I was having my strings pulled."

"If you're angry with us for that," Jessie's voice held no remorse. "We completely understand and accept that. But we are all home in one place as a family again, and I won't apologize for the part I've played in making that happen."

"Neither will I." Oliver clasped his hand through Jessie's in a gesture of unity.

"I thank you for your honesty," Vicky sighed. "I know both your hearts were in the right place." She smiled at them. "We are going to have to put this conversation on hold and order." Her eyes slid towards the door. "Don't turn around. Pick up your menus and choose what you want for dinner."

"Are they here?" Jessie picked up her menu.

"Yes," Vicky nodded, examining her menu. "Take a deep breath and just let the evening flow as if you and Oliver are on a dinner date."

"We are on a dinner date," Jessie said.

"Exactly," Vicky gave her an encouraging smile. "Look, your father won't be looking that hard. But Samantha—there's a lot more to her than meets the eye or the file." She glanced at Jessie and Oliver. "You know the one that you avoided telling me how you got it."

"There is?" Oliver and Jessie said together, surprise widening both their eyes.

"Nothing to concern yourselves with," Vicky told them. "But please, leave Samantha to me. I'll do what is necessary to carry out our plan successfully. But once we have, you and Oliver need to forget about Samantha and destroy or give me any information you may still have on her."

"But..." Jessie began, but Vicky cut her off.

"This is not a negotiation, Jessie!" Vicky's voice was soft but had a hint of iron in it.

"Fine," Jessie sat back and glared at Vicky. "I understand."

"Oliver?" Vicky looked at him questioningly. "Have I made myself clear?"

"Yes, Aunt Vicky," Oliver said respectfully.

"Good," Vicky gave them both one more warning glance. "Now shake off any nerves you have because it's showtime."

Chapter Eight

THE DINNER CRASHERS

The minute Lee stepped into the restaurant, he saw Vicky, and his crazy heart had skipped a few beats. Ever since Vicky had fallen into his arms earlier that afternoon, he hadn't been able to get her out of his mind. No, that was a lie. Since she'd walked into the family dinner to surprise Christy, Lee hadn't been able to get Vicky off his mind.

Lee gave himself a mental shake. What was wrong with him? Was he getting cold feet about Samantha? Lee had been thinking of asking Samantha to marry him for a few months now, long before Vicky had come home. Three months ago, Samantha had started hinting at taking their relationship to another level and how she wasn't getting any younger.

It had taken Lee at least four of those kinds of hints from Samantha before he started thinking that maybe settling down with Samantha would be a good thing. She was beautiful, intelligent, an excellent lawyer, and she wasn't bad company. Lee's relationship with Samantha had been the longest relationship he'd had since Georgia. He was enjoying what they had but also understood that it was time for the relationship to progress or end.

Lee wasn't getting any younger either, and he didn't think he could do much better than the alluring Samantha Harvey.

Besides, they made a good team. But if Lee was brutally honest with himself, he did feel something was missing, and maybe he was stalling about asking Samantha to marry him because of it. Lee had a decision to make because he knew he couldn't string Samantha along forever.

As the waiter led them to their table, they had to pass the table Vicky and Jessie were sitting at.

"Are you following us now?" Vicky grinned up at Lee when they approached their table.

"Vicky!" Lee greeted her. "You remember Samantha?"

"Of course," Vicky's eyes met Samantha's. Vicky had to suppress a shudder as she wondered how brown eyes could look so icy.

"Dad!" Jessie looked up at him, her cheeks flushing in shock like she'd just been caught with her hand in the cookie jar.

"Jessie!" Lee leaned over Oliver to kiss Jessie on the cheek.

When he straightened up, his eyes narrowed as he stared at Oliver, who immediately stood up and held out his hand to Lee. "Hello, sir," Oliver greeted Lee. "I'm Oliver, Jessie's date. Jessie has told me so much about you."

"Oliver?" Lee shook his hand and looked past him towards Jessie. "I can't say my daughter has ever mentioned you."

Oliver frowned at Lee. "I wouldn't have expected her to, sir," he said gallantly. "I'm sure, as you two didn't get much time to spend together when Jessie was studying, that you'd have so much other stuff to talk about."

"You'll have to come for dinner with us some time so we can get to know each other," Lee's invitation sounded like more of a threat.

"I would like that, sir," Oliver said with a slight bow of his head.

"Well, we'll let you get on with your evening," Lee said goodbye and ushered Samantha towards their table, where their waiter was patiently waiting for them.

"Did you know they were going to be here?" Samantha's voice was laced with irritation as Lee held her chair out for her.

"No," Lee said honestly, walking to his seat opposite hers once she was seated. "I did not."

"Do you think they knew we were going to be here?" Samantha's eyes had sparks of anger in them.

"As I didn't tell anyone we were eating here tonight, no, I do not think they knew," Lee assured her.

"I'm sorry," Samantha leaned forward and covered his hand with hers. "I was looking forward to having you all to myself for the evening. We haven't seen each other since the night we were at your family dinner."

"It's been crazy with all my family home…" Lee explained.

"It's not all your fault," Samantha purred, giving him a sultry smile. "I've had a grueling case schedule myself."

"I know," Lee smiled at her. "Let's enjoy our evening. Jessie is having dinner with her friends, so I don't think they'll be bothering us."

"I suppose so," Samantha said as the waiter approached their table.

Lee's eyes slid past Samantha to Jessie's table, and once again, his wayward heart skipped a beat when he saw Vicky laugh at something Jessie was telling her.

"Darling!" Samantha's voice jolted him back to their table. "What beverage do you want?"

Lee ordered a soft drink because he was driving and absently took a menu from the waiter. His eyes skimmed the menu but kept being drawn to Jessie and Vicky's table. Samantha told Lee what she was going to order and, as she spoke, Lee knew in his heart that he wasn't ready to settle down. Not with Samantha, anyway, and it was only fair to tell her so.

Lee was going to wait until he dropped her off at her home later that night. Not that he thought Samantha would resort to it, but he really didn't want a scene at his favorite restaurant. But before he could say anything, their waiter came back with a tray, which he put down on their table while he served their drinks.

Lee's eyes slid to the little blue box on the tray, and something inside him pushed him to ask. "Who's the lucky girl?"

"Table five," the waiter grinned. "The young man had very specific orders to bring the box over with the lady's homemade ginger ale."

Lee's heart froze, and his eyes dropped down to the blue velvet box.

"Do you mean that table over there?" Lee pointed to where Jessie and Vicky were.

"Yes, sir," the waiter confirmed his suspicions. "Is there anything else before I go?"

"Actually..." Lee's eyes narrowed, and irrational anger started to burn in the pit of his stomach. His baby girl was getting engaged without even a hint of warning or him having been formally introduced to her boyfriend. "I'll take that."

Lee snatched the box off the tray before the waiter had time to react.

"No..." The waiter tried to take the box back, but Lee had already scraped his chair back and stood up.

"Lee!" Samantha hissed, looking around the restaurant, embarrassment making her eyes cloud over with anger. "Please, sit down and don't make a scene."

"A scene?" Lee leaned forward, saying softly, "A man I don't even know is about to ask my daughter to marry him. I'm not going to make a scene!" he assured her. "I'm going to rip Oli K's head off!"

Before Samantha had a chance to talk him down, Lee pushed past the waiter that Lee topped by a good foot and marched over to Jessie's table. He slapped the box down on the table and glared at Oliver, who gulped and looked up into Lee's stormy eyes.

"Care to explain this?" Lee hissed.

"Dad!" Jessie breathed, shocked by Lee's behavior. "What are you doing?"

"Wondering why a man I've never met or even knew you were dating before tonight thinks he can propose to my daughter?" Lee's eyes were angry slits when he looked at Jessie.

"Sir, I think you've misunderstood the situation...." Oliver tried to defuse the situation. "It wasn't my intention to propose...."

"Then what is this?" Lee popped the box open and shoved it in Oliver's face.

"Looks like a nice pair of diamond earrings to me!" Vicky said from next to him.

"What?" Lee looked in the box and felt relief swoosh through him. "Earrings?"

"Yes, sir," Oliver nodded. "It's mine and Jessie's anniversary of the day we met today."

"Oli and I always give each other gifts on our anniversary," Jessie said angrily, reaching into her purse and pulling out a box that had gold cufflinks in it. "See?"

"I..." Lee stood there staring at the cufflinks and holding open the box of diamond earrings dumbfounded. "Baby..." His eyes traveled to meet Jessie's blazing ones. "I'm so sorry."

"Thanks, Dad!" Jessie stood up and threw her napkin on the table. "Do you really have so little trust in me that you'd think I would let anyone who hasn't met my dad even think I wanted to marry him?"

"Jess..." Lee snapped the box shut and handed it to Oliver.

"No!" Jessie held up her hand, shaking her head angrily. "Do you know why I introduced Oliver to Aunt Christy and Aunt Vicky first?" Her eyes held her father's. "Because they've been on this side of your scrutiny before, and I was trying to prepare Oliver for meeting you."

"I'm so sorry, Jess," Lee started to move around the table towards her, but she stopped.

"I'm sorry, Dad, but I've had enough!" Jessie bent down and picked up her purse. "I'm sorry, Aunt Vicky, but can we go, please?"

"Yes, if that's what you want?" Vicky stood up and hailed the waiter. "I'll go sort out the bill."

"No, I'll get it," Lee said. "It's the least I can do, having spoiled your evening," he told Vicky. "Jess, can we please just talk?"

"I can't deal with you right now," Jessie told him bluntly. "We can talk in the morning."

Jessie waited for Oliver to get past Lee, "Excuse me, sir," he said and pushed his way towards Jessie. "It was nice to finally meet you," he said politely before Jessie dragged him away.

"We'll meet you in the car," Jessie said to Vicky as she walked past her.

"Jessie!" Lee took off after them.

*V*icky took a deep breath, bent down, and picked up her purse. "Mr. Young is picking up our tab," she told the waiter before following Lee out of the door. "Here we go," she said softly.

Vicky slid a glance towards a fuming Samantha, who was on her phone when Vicky slipped past the table where Samantha was seated and headed towards the door. Her hand shook as she reached for the door handle. Vicky was so angry with Jessie and Oliver that she was finding it very hard to squash the anger that was making her body shake with force.

Jessie and Oliver had completely gone off plan and had implemented the one Vicky had vetoed when Jessie had explained it to her. Jessie had told Vicky that she would bring a date with her to the restaurant and make it seem like her date was going to propose. Jessie thought that Lee would cut his date with Samantha short and not give him time to propose at his shock at hearing the news of his daughter's impending engagement to a man he didn't even know his daughter was dating.

Jessie knew the evening would end with her and Oliver storming out of the restaurant, leaving Vicky to console Lee and get the both of them into a compromising position somewhere, where Samantha would find them. Vicky hadn't wanted to go along with that plan, but Jessie's plan had a few good points. So, Vicky had changed it slightly. Vicky knew Lee was already curious about who Oliver was and that Jessie and Oliver being together at the restaurant would be enough to distract Lee. So, when Lee and Samantha arrived at the restaurant, Vicky would send Lee a message and ask him to meet her outside, so she could tell him what she'd learned about Jessie's relationship.

While they were outside talking, Jessie and Oliver were supposed to talk about how Jessie hoped that Vicky and Lee would end up together. But loud enough that Samantha, who was sitting not far away, would hear. Vicky would keep away from their table for a long enough time for Samantha to grow suspicious and come find them. As soon as Jessie sent the message that Samantha was on her way, Vicky would find a way to end in Lee's arms.

Vicky knew it was not the best plan, but Lee had moved up his plan of getting engaged, and it was all Vicky could come up with at such short notice. So, she'd stolen a leaf out of the old high school playbook of how to break two people up. Make sure one of the couples found the other half in a compromising position with someone else. But Jessie had ambushed Vicky's more subtle plan and dropped a nuclear bomb on Lee. She shook her head as she saw Lee storming towards the parking lot. Vicky nearly twisted her ankle, running after Lee in her high heels.

"Lee!" she called, making him stop and turn towards her. "Let her go!"

"You could've warned me!" Lee said angrily, his green eyes flashing angrily.

"I didn't know until I went to get Jessie," Vicky told him. "I know you're shocked and angry, but I won't stand for you taking this out on me."

Vicky watched Lee clench his fists at his sides, squeeze his eyes shut for a minute, and then slowly open them before running his hand through his hair.

"I'm sorry, Vicky!" Lee took a deep breath. "When I saw that box...."

"Hey," Vicky said softly, walking up to him and touching his arm. "I understand. It must've been such a shock, especially when you were the one going to propose to Samantha tonight."

"I wasn't," Lee shook his head.

"You weren't...?" Vicky gave him a sideways look.

"I wasn't going to propose to Samantha," Lee admitted. "I was going to tell her that I thought our relationship had reached all it was ever going to be."

"You were going to end things with her?" Vicky looked at him, amazed.

"Well, not at first," Lee told her. "It wasn't until I walked into the restaurant and saw you and Jessie laughing and enjoying yourselves that I realized that I had been looking for every excuse I could to not propose to Samantha."

"I..." Vicky's eyes locked with Lee's.

Vicky honestly didn't know who took the first step towards the other before she felt Lee's lips crush hers, and the next thing she knew, their arms were entwined around each other.

"Lee!" Samantha's angry voice had them jumping apart guiltily.

"Samantha..." Lee stepped protectively in front of Vicky.

"What is going on?" Samantha's angry eyes traveled from Lee to Vicky.

"We need to talk," Lee told her. "I didn't mean for this to happen like this, though."

"Are you breaking up with me?" Samantha looked genuinely shocked. "Here?"

"I didn't want to do it here in an alley," Lee assured her. "Can I take you home, and we can talk on the way?"

"No, don't bother," Samantha gave Vicky a searing look. "I'll find my own way home."

Samantha spun on her three-inch heels and stormed off.

"Vicky..." Lee turned back towards her. "Can we talk tomorrow?" His voice was soft and filled with emotion. "I need to try and catch Samantha." He looked at her. "I'm sorry."

Vicky couldn't believe how hard her heart was beating. Or how much she really wanted to feel his arms around her again. It took everything Vicky had to smile up at him and lift herself onto her toes to reach up and kiss him on the cheek. "Goodnight, Lee," she said and started to walk to her car. "Good luck with Samantha."

"Goodnight, Vicky," Lee's voice was hoarse.

Vicky didn't have to look back to know he was watching her; she could feel it. As she climbed into her car, she knew without a shadow of a doubt Lee wasn't the only one that was watching her.

"I see that went well," Jessie said, sliding her safety belt on.

Vicky could see the slight shake of Jessie's hand and knew that Jessie knew she'd messed up. Jessie was also pale and wide-eyed with shock.

"Jessie, what were you thinking?" Vicky asked angrily, giving Oliver an angry glare as well. She needed to make sure both Jessie and Oliver knew just how cross she was that they had gone off the plan. "Jess, I told you we were going to do this my way tonight." Her eyes narrowed.

"I know..." Jessie looked at Vicky. "I'm sorry, Aunt Vicky. I should've listened to you but...."

"But you didn't trust that I would be able to play my part in what was supposed to happen tonight?" Vicky shook her head in disbelief. "For someone so intelligent, what you did tonight was beyond stupid."

"Yes, I know," Jessie's voice was filled with remorse. "I just thought...."

"I'm sorry, Jessie," Vicky started the car and slowly backed out of the parking lot before turning into the street. "Breaking off your father's relationship like we had planned to do was not nice. But what you did tonight was reprehensible, you completely disregarded everything I warned you about, and you undermined me."

"I will make things right with my father," Jessie promised.

"But on a positive side, we stopped my father from making the biggest mistake of his life in proposing to the wrong woman."

"Yes, but the way it was done was brutal," Vicky stopped at a traffic light and glanced in the mirror. The car that had been following them was still behind them. "Honey, you need to set things right with your father first thing in the morning."

"I will, I promise," Jessie told Vicky. "I knew he'd be upset about me having a boyfriend and seeing that box, but I never in a million years thought he'd react like he did."

"How did you think he'd react when he saw a box that looked like a ring box being taken to our table?" Vicky glanced at Jessie, who looked down at her hands.

"I don't know." Jessie looked out the passenger window. "I thought he'd ask me to have a private word outside, maybe. Even if he came to the table to ask what was going on, I was going to ask him and Samantha to join us at the table so that I could explain about Oliver." She looked back down at her hand. "I thought if I could get him to our table, I could keep him from proposing tonight and give you time to implement your Plan A."

"Jessie knew you were reluctant to have to get her father into a compromising position so Samantha could catch you," Oliver explained for Jessie. "We were trying not to jeopardize yours and Lee's relationship by making you do something you were uncomfortable with."

"While I appreciate the sentiment," Vicky told them both. "You never poke a bear, especially when it's going through something painful." She sighed. "Honey, your father's been a single parent since you had just learned to walk," her voice was filled with compassion. "After what happened with you and Ian...." She sighed. "I knew the minute I saw the waiter with that little blue box that you were lighting a flame beneath a powder keg."

"Aunt Vicky's right," Oliver backed Vicky up. "If I were in your father's shoes tonight, I probably would've reacted just the same way, where my only daughter was concerned." He reached over the front seat and put his hand lovingly on Jessie's shoulder. "I should've realized that sooner and talked you out of this plan.

You and I should both know the lengths our parents will go to to protect us."

"Oliver's right, Jess," Vicky told her. "Your father would go to any lengths to protect you. Just like you've just done for him tonight." She blew out a breath. "But now, we are going to have to do damage control because Lee thinks that he's the one in the wrong." She glanced at Jessie. "So, I know I can count on you to make it up to him."

"But without letting him know we set him up, right?" Jessie looked over at Vicky. Her eyes were wide and pleading.

"For now, until we know what Samantha is going to do," Vicky told her. "I don't think your father needs to know our part in the breakup."

"You mean what I did to him!" Jessie said emphatically. "I ambushed you with my plan as much as I blindsided my father tonight. So, I take full responsibility for what happened tonight."

Vicky thought it was admirable of Jessie wanting to shoulder the blame for scheming against Lee. But Vicky also knew that deep in her heart, she'd probably do something similar all over again if she had to. Vicky also knew that a small part of her was relieved when Jessie had defied her warnings and implemented her plan instead. It meant that Vicky didn't have to instigate a compromising position with Lee because Vicky was much better at consoling Lee than she was at seducing him.

"We!" Vicky reminded Jessie. "What we did to your dad. We were all in this together and, as much as it pained me to do that to someone, I...." She caught herself before saying love. "Care about. I know we needed to get him out of Samantha Harvey's clutches. I might not agree with the methods that were used, but I could've put a stop to the shenanigans at any time, and I didn't." She looked at Jessie and gave her an encouraging smile. "By doing that, I become an accessory to your manipulation plot."

"We did the wrong thing for the right reasons," Olive said. "Sometimes we have to do whatever it takes to protect the people we love."

Vicky knew what Oliver had said was true and that they had succeeded in breaking off the relationship between Lee and Samantha. But Vicky's emotions were torn. She hated having manipulated Lee the way they had. But Vicky couldn't help feeling that she'd wanted Lee's relationship to end for more than just to protect him. And that feeling was wrapping her in an ugly blanket of guilt.

Chapter Nine

THE GUEST HIDDEN IN THE BASEMENT

Lee woke up with a start. He glanced around his room with his heart beating in his throat. The sun's rays were trying to squeeze in between the small gaps in the drapes. Lee glanced at his bedside clock and suddenly came fully awake when he realized what the time was. He had a big day ahead of him both at work and at home. Lee sighed and pinched the bridge of his nose as the events for the past two days swirled through his mind.

After the night at the restaurant, Lee had gone into work the next day, hoping to get a chance to talk to Samantha. She hadn't been taking his calls or answering his messages. Not that Lee could blame her. It was never his intention for Samantha to have been humiliated or find out he wanted to end their relationship the way she did. Lee was still appalled by his behavior and at what he'd done and knew he owed Samantha an apology.

But when he'd got to work the next day, it was to find out that Samantha had quit the DA's office without warning or giving any reason. She'd sent their boss an email, telling him that she wouldn't be in on that day or ever again. That wasn't the first shock that Lee had gotten that day. A few hours after Lee was told about Samantha, his brother Justin had knocked on his door, and he had not been alone. Justin was with a man from the FBI, Special Agent Garry.

They were there to question Lee about Samantha. At first, Lee was stunned and immediately thought something must've happened to Samantha. His stomach had dropped, and his mind flashed back to when Georgia had disappeared and how he'd become the number one suspect for her disappearance. It wouldn't look good if yet another woman in Lee's life had disappeared, or worse, wound up dead.

But Justin and Garry were there to talk about the fact that the real Samantha Harvey, who was an attorney, had died in prison seven years ago. The woman that Lee had worked with and been in a serious relationship with for the past year was not Samantha Harvey. Garry believed that Lee had been targeted by the fake Samantha for a reason. To that end, Lee was now working with Special Agent Garry to go through all of Lee's cases, going back for at least two years.

Lee also had a feeling that he was secretly being interrogated to find out if he'd been involved with whatever Samantha was up to. The past two days since the dinner fiasco had passed by in a blur of activity, and Lee hadn't had time to process the shock of what was actually happening. Nor had he had time to ponder over what had happened between Vicky and him outside the restaurant that night. Images of the kiss seared his mind, and his heart raced. He could still taste her on his lips and feel how good it felt to hold her in his arms. Lee swallowed and pushed himself out of bed. He had to get up, or he was going to be late for work. Today was the day he was handing in his resignation at the DA's office.

Lee had decided to take Shaun Donovan up on his offer to take over Donovan Law. The moment Lee knew he couldn't ask Samantha to marry him and that he wanted to end their relationship, Lee knew he was going to accept Shaun's offer. It was one of Lee's goals in life to have his own law firm, and he knew he'd been lucky to get an offer of a lifetime like he had from Shaun Donovan. Shaun's law firm was well known and established.

As Lee wandered into his bathroom, his mind went over a million reasons why Samantha had targeted him. Maybe it had nothing to do with one of his cases and more to do with someone in his family. Lee's thoughts alarmed him, and he made a mental note to call Justin on his way to work and see if his brother could meet him before work. He needed to run his latest thoughts about Samantha Harvey by Justin.

As Lee went about getting ready, his mind drifted back to the dinner and the kiss he'd shared with Vicky. His heart did a double skip, and his hand shook slightly, putting toothpaste on his toothbrush. Lee hadn't seen or heard from Vicky since the night at the restaurant, and he knew that he had to go and speak to her soon. Then there was Jessie! His daughter had moved into the pool house with her cousin Mya the previous day. She had come and apologized to him for springing Oliver on him like that.

Lee had had a good talk with her last night when he'd gotten home from work, and they'd sorted things out. Oliver was coming over for dinner tomorrow. Lee knew he hadn't made a good first impression on the young man, but then again, the young man hadn't exactly made a good one on Lee either. He knew he'd overreacted to the whole Oliver proposing thing, but at the end of the day, Jessie and Oliver had been wrong to be sneaking around for the past five years.

Lee's mind flashed back to Samantha as he got dressed. He couldn't believe he'd dated her for as long as he had without suspecting a thing. It just proved that no one ever really gets to know a person. You could have endless hours of conversations with them about their lives and who they were. But when it all came down to it, you were really just taking what they were telling you as the truth. Unless you did a complete background check on a person every time you met them, you were never truly going to know if they were lying about who they were.

Vicky, however, Lee had known her whole life. She'd been at their dinner table nearly every night when they were growing up. Lee was pretty sure he knew Vicky very well, although he did pick up that she was a little more guarded lately. He frowned. But that was probably because she had a lot on her mind with having only lost Grant a few years ago and then moving back home to Key West from Miami. And she was funny, she told it like she saw it, and there was never a dull moment with her. Vicky also knew him very well and had been his first love.

Lee's heart thudded erratically once again as he thought about the kiss they'd shared the other night. He smiled into the mirror while putting on his tie. Who knew? Maybe Vicky would be the one he'd grow old with. No, not maybe; Lee knew he'd fallen in love with her again. The moment she'd walked back into his family home, his heart had responded to her and had been reaching out for her ever since. The way she'd kissed him back showed that she felt something for him too.

"Lee," Christy's voice called from the front door. "Have you got a minute?"

"I'll be right there," Lee called back from his bedroom, picked up his suit jacket, put on his watch, and took his wallet from his bedside drawer before walking into the living room. "Good morning. Is everything okay?"

"Yes..." Christy bit her lip and fiddled with her phone. "Actually, no." She shook her head.

"What's wrong?" Lee's eyes widened with worry.

"Here," Christy said, handing him her phone with a message open on it. "What are we going to do?"

Lee took the phone and read the message. His brows raised up in surprise when he saw who the message was from.

Hi Christy, I know it's been a long time, and I'm probably the last person you thought to hear from. But I'm coming home in the next two weeks or at least before Christmas. And this time, it's for real and for good. I'm dying to see my family and

*especially Hannah. I have a lot to
explain to my baby girl and to you
all. I'm sorry I can't say more, but
I have to go.
Love Matty xx*

"Do you think she's serious this time?" Lee handed Christy's phone back to her.

"I don't know," Christy said. "Hannah asked me about Matty about a week ago. It was completely out of the blue." She looked at Lee wide-eyed. "You don't think Matty's been in touch with Hannah directly, do you?"

"Don't you monitor Hannah's social media and phone?" Lee asked.

"No, not anymore. I allowed her to get onto social media when she turned fourteen because she was good with her phone," Christy explained. "I don't want to invade her privacy."

"That's admirable of you," Lee told her. "Then the only way you're going to find out if Hannah has had contact with Matty recently is to ask her."

"I know," Christy bit her lip again. "Do I tell Hannah about this message?"

"I think you should." Lee put a fresh pot of coffee on. "Hannah is fifteen now, and it's better to have told her than let her find out some other way."

"You're right." Christy declined Lee's offer of a coffee. "I have to get to work. Mya is taking Hannah to school on her way to work."

"How are Mya and Aaron getting on?" Lee asked, getting his coffee mug ready.

"They are going to some hockey game together tonight and taking Hannah, Luke, and Jessie," Christy told Lee. "They did ask me along, but I think it's good for Aaron to bond with all of our kids." She smiled. "Mya told me two days ago that she wished she'd decided to find out who her father was earlier. That she'd secretly always wanted to but felt she was somehow betraying Dustin, who always will be her dad."

"I know Aaron can't believe he has a daughter and has already started to do the proud father bragging thing." Lee grinned.

"I've noticed that," Christy shook her head. "Can you imagine if he'd known about her when she was younger?"

"Oh, yes!" Lee laughed. "Mya had a way of wrapping everyone around her little finger. I can only imagine how she'd have led Aaron around."

"Well, she's making up for lost time," Christy told Lee. "The other day, Aaron asked me if it was okay to get Mya, Hannah, Jessie, and Luke a new car for Christmas."

"What did you say?" Lee took a sip of coffee.

"That I never spoiled Mya or Luke, I'd like to think that they appreciated everything they had. Because they either had to work for it or knew how hard someone else had to be able to give it to them." Christy sighed. "To which Aaron replied that he had thirty years to make up for."

"Let me guess, you buckled because of your big heart that felt sorry for Aaron?" Lee sighed.

"Yes," Christy confirmed Lee's suspicion. "But I've since seen the car he wants to buy for them to share," she raised her eyebrows. "Let's just say there are going to be three very happy people in our house on Christmas day."

"Great!" Lee rolled his eyes. "How do we top a gift like that?"

"I'm not sure," Christy said honestly. "I haven't even thought about Christmas presents yet."

"No, neither have I, to be honest," Lee finished his coffee and rinsed his cup out. "Are you going to reply to Matty?"

Lee brought the topic back to the message Christy had gotten from the youngest of the Young siblings. Their sister, who had gone off on an assignment, left her five-year-old daughter in Christy's care and disappeared.

"I will," Christy said. "I'm just trying to figure out what to say."

"I better get to the office." Lee noticed the time on the kitchen clock. "Keep me updated about Matty."

"I will," Christy promised, walking out of the cottage with Lee. "I'll see you later. Have a good day."

"You too, Christy," Lee said to his sister and headed for his car.

Well, that was another unexpected turn of events, Lee thought as he pulled out of the drive and headed towards his office. There were a few good things to come from the events of the night at the restaurant. Lee had decided to start steering his life back on track and ticking off the goals he'd set for himself before Georgia disappeared. As soon as he handed in his resignation at the DA's office, he was on his way to fulfilling at least one of them.

When Lee pulled up at the office, he toyed with the idea of inviting Vicky to dinner tomorrow night. By the time Lee was settled at his desk in his office, he'd made up his mind to take the plunge and send the invite. Lee took out his phone and messaged Vicky.

> *Hi! Would you like to have dinner with me tomorrow night?*

Lee put the phone down on his desk and started to go through his caseload for the day. It wasn't more than fifteen minutes later when his phone beeped. Lee looked down at his phone and smiled. Vicky had replied.

> *If you're buying? I'm in. What time and where?*

Lee sat back in his chair and thought for a few minutes before coming up with an idea.

> *How about my house, seven-thirty, and I'll order in from your favorite*

He sent the message, and Vicky replied.

Sounds good. I'll bring the wine! Don't forget the caramel cheesecake dessert!

Lee laughed.

I would never forget the cheesecake!

Vicky responded instantly once again.

Good, I'll see you tomorrow night.

Lee stared at the messages between them for another few minutes before his assistant knocked on his office door to remind him of his first appointment for the day.

*V*icky knocked on Christy's office door and entered before Christy could answer.

"Hi!" Vicky gave Christy a wave as she walked into her office, carrying two cups of Christy's favorite iced coffees and two cream cheese bagels.

"Vicky!" Christy looked up from her paperwork and smiled. "What a lovely surprise." She saw the food and cups in Vicky's hands. "Is that…?"

"Your favorite iced coffee and a cream cheese bagel from It Has To Be A Bagel," Vicky said and handed them over to Christy. "I thought you could use some lunch."

"You're a lifesaver," Christy thanked Vicky. "I skipped breakfast this morning and was just thinking I'd need to send someone out to get me lunch as I'm snowed under here today."

"Well, then I'm glad I came bearing food." Vicky took a seat in a chair facing Christy's desk and fiddled with her bagel. "I didn't only come to make sure you got some food in you." She licked some cream cheese off her fingers.

"Ah," Christy's eyes narrowed as she stirred her iced coffee and opened her bagel. "So, this is bribe food?"

"I guess you can look at it like that," Vicky grinned. "I have something to tell you, and if you're uncomfortable with what I have to say, I'll back out."

"Uh, oh!" Christy halved her bagel. "The last time you said something along those lines, you made me go on a double date with the cousin of the guy you had a crush on."

"Yes, and I've apologized for that for the last thirty-two years!" Vicky rolled her eyes. "I promise this has nothing to do with double dating...." She frowned. "Or at least, not yet."

"Oh..." Christy sat back in her chair with a half bagel in her hand. "Does this have something to do with my oldest brother?" She grinned at Vicky, whose cheeks heated up guiltily.

"The other night..." Vicky swallowed. "The night he broke up with Samantha and had a falling out with Jessie, we shared a...."

"Kiss?" Christy asked.

"How did you...?" Vicky's brows drew together, and her eyes narrowed.

"Jessie told me," Christy said and smiled.

"Why, that little snitch!" Vicky took a bite of her bagel.

"She's very happy, by the way, as she thinks there is something between you and Lee," Christy took a bite of her bagel and, when she was finished chewing, asked, "is there?"

"I don't know," Jessie said honestly. "I have something else to admit to you about myself and Lee." Vicky swallowed.

"Oh?" Christy looked at Vicky expectantly.

"When I was sixteen, we had another moment," Vicky admitted. "I had a huge crush on Lee, and I was having a bad day; he comforted me, we kissed, and then I told him it could never happen again because my friendship with you was everything to me."

"I always thought you were crazy for pushing him away like you did back then." Christy sighed.

"You knew?" Vicky looked at Christy accusingly.

"Of course, I did," Christy admitted. "You're my best friend, Vicky. I always knew when you liked someone."

"It's just as well we didn't start dating because he would've broken my heart when he met Georgia," Vicky said, taking another bite of her food.

"Or you and Lee might've gotten married!" Christy pointed out.

"Why didn't you say anything back then?" Vicky asked.

"I knew you were protecting our friendship, and everything blew up with Shannon and me, and then Lee met Georgia." Christy leaned forward and picked up her coffee. "And then you moved on as well."

"Now that that part's out of the way…" Vicky scrunched up her nose as if she was about to rip a band-aid off sensitive skin. "Lee asked me over to his house tomorrow night for dinner."

"I hope you accepted, and I hope he's getting takeout," Christy grinned at the look Vicky gave her. "What? Neither you nor Lee can cook!"

"Yes, Lee is getting take-out," Vicky assured Christy, rolling her eyes. "Do you think I should tell Jessie?"

"I think that's an admirable thing to do," Christy told Vicky. "It also shows her that you respect her relationship with her father."

"I agree," Vicky said. "Are you sure you're okay with me going on a date with Lee?"

"I couldn't be happier," Christy promised Vicky. "I couldn't think of anyone better for my brother than my best friend. And I couldn't think of anyone better for my best friend than my big brother."

"Thank you, that means a lot to me," Vicky told Christy. "How are things going with you and Aaron?"

"Very well," Christ said, her eyes sparkling when she thought of Aaron. "Who would've thought the both of us would circle back to our first loves?"

"I guess some relationships are just destined to be even if it takes decades to come full circle," Vicky reasoned. "But, let's not get ahead of ourselves with Lee and me. It's our first dinner date, and we've only kissed once."

"Twice!" Christy held up two fingers.

"That doesn't really count anymore as it was years and years ago," Vicky reasoned.

"Nope," Christy took another sip of her iced coffee. "It still counts."

"This does feel a little weird," Vicky said.

"I know... I feel like I'm prying into my brother's love life." Christy grinned.

"Are you sure this isn't going to be awkward?" Vicky asked.

"Vicky..." Christy's eyes narrowed. "Are you trying to talk yourself out of going to dinner with Lee?"

"No!" Vicky scrunched up her face. "Why would you think that?"

"Because I can see the wheels turning in your head," Christy told her. "And no, I don't think it will be awkward at all. I told you I've always secretly hoped you and Lee would find your way back to each other."

"Thank you," Vicky finished her bagel. "I feel a lot better now that you know I'm having dinner with Lee."

"I feel a lot better that he's no longer dating Samantha," Christy said honestly. "Especially now that the DA's office has found out that she had stolen the identity of a dead woman."

"Excuse me?" Vicky was about to take a sip of her iced coffee but stopped with the cup halfway to her mouth. "What's happened to Samantha?"

"Nothing, she's in the wind." Christy picked up the other half of her bagel. "There's now an investigation going on at the DA's office."

"I can imagine," Vicky said. "It's a serious crime to impersonate a lawyer?"

"Yes." Christy nodded. "Then, to top it all, Lee and I got another shock this morning."

"Another shock?" Vicky asked.

"Yes," Christy said, picking up her phone. She scrolled through it and put it in front of Vicky open on a message. "I got this from Matty this morning."

"Do you think she means it this time?" Vicky asked Christy, giving back her phone. "Matty has said she's coming home a few times in the past but hasn't."

"I think this time she's actually going to come home," Christy said. "I think Matty may also have been in contact with Hannah through social media."

"Would you like me to check for you?" Vicky asked her.

"No, I'm going to ask Hannah tonight when I'm home from work," Christy explained to Vicky. "I know Hannah. I think if I ask her, she'll tell me the truth of what I want to know."

"You've always been such an amazing mother," Vicky complimented her.

"Thank you." Christy smiled. "I always thought if I could be half the mother that my mother was, that I would be doing a good job."

"Your mother was the best," Vicky agreed.

"I still miss her each and every single day," Christy told Vicky, her eyes misted over.

"I do too. As far as I was concerned, Aunt Lucy was my mother too." Vicky said, a lump burning in the back of her throat.

"I know!" Christy smiled. "Oh goodness, is that the time?" She looked at her wristwatch. "Sorry, Vicky, thank you for the lunch, but I have a meeting."

"I'd better get going anyway," Vicky said. "I have to approve the new website for the dance studio as well as go over the schedule with all my new dance instructors."

"I'm so glad you're home, Vicky," Christy smiled at her.

"I'll walk with you," Vicky said and walked out of the office with Christy. "Keep me updated about Matty."

"I will," Christy promised.

They said goodbye, and Vicky walked out of the station towards her car. Before she got to it, she opened the back door and made a show of putting her purse behind her.

"You know, we really have to stop doing this!" Vicky before closing the back door and climbing into the driver's seat.

"But it adds to the air of romance!" the man said. "I've managed to find a way for you to talk to Roberta Davies."

"Have you found out what or who the target may have been after?" Vicky started her car and pulled out of the parking lot.

"Not yet," he admitted. "Although, Lee Young thinks it might be someone close to him, maybe even a family member."

"Ah," Vicky nodded. "Speaking of family members, have you managed to track down our escapee yet?"

"Jeez, what do you think I am? A machine?" he grumbled. "You've got me working all over the place here, V."

"So, where is our escapee?" Vicky sighed and shook her head. He could be so melodramatic.

"Not sure yet," He took an apple out of his jacket, and Vicky looked at him in disgust. "But I'll find them."

"Seriously?" Vicky looked at him. "You've been in my house, again!"

"You always have the best fruit," he complimented. "But I went in there because I saw someone else going in there."

"Was it perhaps my father?" Vicky asked him sarcastically. "Because he does live there too, you know!"

"You know you told me you kept feeling like you were being watched, especially when you were in your neighborhood?"

"Yes," Vicky said with a frown.

"Well, I think one of the people who've been watching you is actually squatting in your basement," he shocked her with the information.

"What?" Vicky raised her voice in shock. Her head shot up to the mirror so fast to look at him in the back seat that she nearly drove them off the road.

"Hey...." He grabbed onto the seat. "Should I use the other seat belts at the back here, too?"

"Sorry," Vicky said. "Who was in my house?"

"The same person you asked me to look into," he told her. "You know, V, you really need to be more vigilant. Since you've been back in Key West, you've been really lax with your security."

"I would've known!" Vicky assured him. "If I have a squatter, they moved into the basement today."

"No, they didn't," he threw an envelope of photos on the passenger seat. "Your squatter has been living in your basement for a good two months or so." He pointed to the photos he'd taken from Vicky's house. "I found these down there. All taken within the past few months right up to you coming home to Key West."

"No way!" Vicky's eyes widened in fright. "My father was living there on his own then!"

"Oh, don't worry about your father," the man began. "Turns out your father knows about the squatter."

"My father's been hiding..." Vicky's jaw clenched, and she drew in a deep, calming breath. "First thing in the morning, you need to find a new home for my basement guest."

"Oh, no!" He shook his head and held up his hands. "No! No way." He looked at her in the mirror. "There's no room at the Inn!"

"I know for a fact there's space at the Inn." Vicky gave him a smug smile.

"Seriously, V," he pointed his apple at her. "You're lucky I owe you."

"I'm also lucky enough to know that you're not doing this because you owe me," Vicky said softly. "You're doing this because you're a decent person."

"Uh-huh," he said. "We both know there are a *lot* of people who would argue with that."

"None of us have squeaky clean hands!" Vicky shrugged and pulled up at a different recycling place than the one she'd dropped him at before. "What I really want to know now is why I wasn't immediately contacted about Samantha being in the wind?" Vicky looked into the rearview mirror. "The agency obviously knows already that she's disappeared, and the DA's office has found out she was a fraud. Yet they haven't said a word to me or changed the mission status."

"So far, it's been working in our favor," he pointed out. "But I'll find out what I can," he promised her.

"Be careful; you're back out in the open now," Vicky warned him. "Oh... and...." She leaned over and picked up his recycling. "I'm not your garbage collector."

Vicky climbed out of her car, leaving her driver's door open to give him cover to slip away.

"It makes for such a great cover, though." He grinned before stealthily sliding out of the car and disappearing between two buildings.

Vicky sighed as she got rid of his recycling before climbing back into her car and heading home. She looked at her wristwatch. She knew her father went home every day at around this time to get his lunch. Vicky was sure her dad's hidden house guest would be joining him for lunch. That was why Vicky parked her car near Young House before sneaking inside her own house through the back glass sliding door.

Vicky heard voices coming from the dining room. She quietly made her way towards the room, stopping just outside the door to listen. Her brows drew together when she heard a female voice. Vicky froze. It was a voice she knew and one that shouldn't be in her house. Vicky gave a silent sigh and shook her head. *What are you three up to?*

"Uncle Shaun, you have to let me see her!" Vicky heard the female voice say. "We could possibly solve this case once and for all. Then we can all finally stop looking over our shoulders."

"I know you want this to end, honey," Vicky heard her dad's calm, level voice. "I've already gone over and beyond to get her here. I'm sure by now Vicky's figured out what's...."

"What has Vicky figured out, Dad?" Vicky stepped into the

dining room, surprising all three of them, who each looked up at her in shock. "Hello." She folded her arms, and her eyes narrowed as she looked at the woman who Vicky assumed must be her basement squatter. "Looks like the prodigal child really has returned."

"Vicky!" The person in question stood up and faced Vicky. "I can explain...."

"Oh, you're going to do that, alright!" Vicky pulled out her phone.

"What are you doing?" Shaun Donovan looked wearily at his daughter. "Vicky, you don't know what's going on here."

"I think I'm beginning to get the big picture!" Vicky raised her eyebrows at Shaun.

"Who are you calling?" The woman eyed Vicky suspiciously. "Vicky, no one can know about this."

Something made Vicky cancel the call she was about to make to get her basement squatter extracted right away. "Then you'd better start explaining to me what's going on, or I'll start making calls to relocate our surprise houseguest."

"Vicky, you need to let this one go..." Shaun tried to reason with his daughter.

"No, Dad!" Vicky said, shaking her head. "I don't think either of you understand." She looked at the woman. "Your secret houseguest has attracted the attention of a Black Widow."

"What?" Shaun asked.

"Let's just say you don't want to find out," Vicky hissed.

"And it's not just any Black Widow either," she told them. "So, whatever is going on here needs to be explained to me in full." She warned the two of them, "And know this, if I catch so much of a hint either of you are lying to me or still keeping something from me after you've each had a turn to explain this to me, I won't be relocating just our houseguest."

"I understand," the woman said softly. "You have our full cooperation."

"You don't have to do this!" Shaun looked at their houseguest.

"No, Uncle Shaun." The woman turned to look at him. "Vicky is right." She swallowed. "This situation is a lot more serious than we possibly know." She looked at Vicky, her brow furrowed as she asked, "By Black Widow, I take it you don't mean the actual spider?" the houseguest asked. Her eyes were huge with fear.

"No," Vicky said. "It's a lot worse."

"Are you talking about that group of alleged assassins?" Shaun looked at his daughter in disbelief. "Honey, they're nothing but a myth."

"No, Dad, they are not."

"Assassins?" The woman's eyes widened.

"They are a group of what are called erasers," Shaun explained. "Which is a nice way of saying deadly assassins."

"Which not only puts a target on your back," Vicky looked at the houseguest. "But your family and most probably anyone in our neighborhood or who gets in the way of them accomplishing whatever their mission is."

Chapter Ten

A UNIQUE FIRST DATE

Vicky had butterflies in her stomach. She had also changed her outfit at least six times before settling on jeans and a soft cotton shirt. Her houseguest, whom Vicky had decided to let stay at her house so she could personally keep an eye on, had been delighted to find out about Vicky's date. She had also been instrumental in helping Vicky pick out her outfit.

Thinking of her houseguest brought up problems that Vicky could deal with tomorrow. Tonight, she was going to take her best friend Christy's advice and enjoy herself. But as Vicky walked the short distance from her house to Lee's, she once again felt she was being watched. Only this time, she knew it wasn't her houseguest, and Vicky had a pretty good idea who else it might be.

As Vicky walked, she listened and knew she was being followed. She turned the corner when she reached the Young house and stopped, waiting. When the person turned the corner, Vicky acted quickly and pinned her stalker to the wall.

"I knew it was you!" Vicky said into the person's ear. "What is your game?"

"I'm not who you think I am!" the person hissed. "If you stop trying to break my arm, I'll explain."

"How about I apply more pressure every second you're not

talking," Vicky put more pressure on the arms she was twisting. "You can start by telling me who hired you and what your connection to Robin Kelly is?"

"Robin is trying to help me," the person surprised Vicky by saying. "In exchange, I promised to help her and you."

"You're lying!" Vicky hissed. "What could we possibly need your help with?"

"For starters, I know that you're looking into Key West Research Labs, and I have information about that and the mysterious client of your father's," Vicky's prisoner told her.

"Why would I believe anything you have to say?" Vicky hissed. "You nearly killed a good friend of mine, and you were targeting another." She gave the person's arm another little twist. "I've also since found out that my agency sent me bogus information about you. Why would that be?"

"I can explain that too," the person winced as Vicky tightened her grip.

"You have one minute to convince me, Samantha...." Vicky sneered. "Or, shall I say Cordelia Watson?"

"Cordelia Watson is dead!" She said, "And the real Samantha Harvey was my sister."

Vicky froze. "Samantha Harvey was killed in prison and was in there for murder."

"No, Samantha was falsely accused of murder and deliberately thrown into the wrong prison to make sure she'd end up dead so no one could learn what she'd found out."

Vicky stepped back and let Samantha or whatever she was calling herself now free. "You expect me to believe that you, of all people, have turned from killing people to helping them because you grew a heart when your sister was killed?"

"No, but I hope you'll believe me," Robin Kelly's soft voice had Vicky spinning around.

"Robin, you have a lot of explaining to do," Vicky said.

"I know," Robin said, holding up her hands. "But please, you need to hear us out."

"Right, now, Robin," Vicky glared at her. "You need to

take..." She looked at the other woman, "Whoever she is now, and meet me at the dance studio in three hours."

"Stephanie Harvey," Robin told Vicky. "That's her real name."

"I gathered as much," Vicky said. "Why would you take your real name?"

"Everyone thinks I'm dead," Stephanie told Vicky. "So, I figured as I'm a ghost, I may as well be one with my real name."

"Three hours!" Vicky looked from Stephanie to Robin. "Before you think of doing anything cute...." She pointed to Stephanie's chest where a small red dot was. "Know that you're both being watched."

"Touché!" Stephanie said to Vicky.

"Now go before I change my mind and take you both in myself," Vicky looked from Stephanie to Robin.

When Robin and Stephanie walked off towards Robin's house, Vicky said, "Keep an eye on them." She didn't need an answer from him because she knew he could hear her. "Oh, and I'll be leaving my coat in the hall, so you can't eavesdrop on my date." She let him know she'd found his little device.

"I'm sorry I'm late," Vicky said when Lee let her in.

Lee helped her with her coat. "You're not late at all." He hung her coat up on the rack next to his front door and took the bottle of wine she handed him. "Come on in and make yourself at home."

Vicky walked with Lee into the living room. "I like what you've done with the place."

"It's a lot better than it was when I was a student." Lee laughed. "But most of the decorating is thanks to my sisters and daughter."

"What's it like having Ty living next door to you?" Vicky asked him.

"We hardly see each other," Lee admitted. "But he's a quiet neighbor who loves to stick his nose in my business."

"That's only because he cares!" Vicky watched Lee open the bottle of wine she'd brought and pour some into two glasses, one of which he handed to her. "The food smells good."

"I put it in the oven to keep it warm," Lee told her. "Would you like to eat now? Or I have some pre-dinner snacks in the living room."

"Living room, it is," Vicky said. "My father is very excited that you've finally accepted his offer." She said, sitting on the sofa.

"I'm excited about it as well," Lee told her, taking a seat next to her. "I handed in my resignation yesterday."

"How did that go down?" Vicky asked him.

"Not too well now that Samantha, or whoever she is, left the DA's office high and dry." Lee took a sip of his wine. "Help yourself to snacks," he offered.

"I will because you've got all my favorite entrees here," Vicky looked at the assortment of crackers, cheeses, olives, and grapes. "Christy mentioned that. She also mentioned that you were helping the FBI with finding her."

"I've been scouring all of my cases from two years ago with the agent," Lee told Vicky. "But to date, we've not found anything that we can see she'd be interested in."

"What about the case of the woman whose name she was using?" Vicky asked Lee.

"Samantha Harvey?" Lee frowned.

"Yes," Vicky nodded. "Do you think maybe the fake Samantha was trying to find information on the person's identity she was using?"

"That would be risky, wouldn't it?" Lee frowned. "I don't think that case was here in Key West." He leaned forward and took a cracker. "Samantha was in prison in Ocala, at Lowell Correctional Institution."

"Did anyone look into where her case was tried?" Vicky asked. "And who at the DA offices where you work hired the fake Samantha?" Vicky asked.

"Judge Harkem introduced her to the previous DA," Lee told Vicky.

"Where are the previous DA and the judge now?" Vicky looked at Lee questioningly.

"Judge Harkem and the previous DA are both retired, and as far as I know, they live in the same retirement village as Pops," Lee said before taking another sip of his wine.

"Have you looked into the connection between the three of them?" Vicky took a sip of her wine.

"That's a good idea," Lee admitted. "I'll speak to Special Agent Garry in the morning."

"I've got an even better idea!" Vicky grinned. "Why don't we go visit them right now?"

"Now?" Lee looked up at the clock on the wall. "It's almost eight."

"It's still early," Vicky said. "Come on."

"Why is it that every time I'm with you, I end up doing the craziest things?" Lee rolled his eyes.

"You mean adventurous things, right?" Vicky put her wine glass down on the coffee table. "Come on; we'll be gone for an hour, max. I'm sure the food will still be okay when we get back."

"Or," Lee said, looking up at her. "We could wait until the morning and then go visit them."

"I happen to know that there are dance lessons happening at the retirement village right now," Vicky told him. "Compliments of Vicky's Dance Studio."

"So, you think that they're at the dance lessons?" Lee looked up at her.

"Uh-huh," Vicky nodded. "I know this because only three people didn't sign up, and it wasn't the judge or the ex-DA."

"You're not going to make me dance, are you?" Lee sighed and pushed himself to his feet.

"We'll see," Vicky said. "I make no promises in that department."

"Fine!" Lee reluctantly followed Vicky to the front door, where they grabbed their coats, and Lee picked up his keys.

"I think I have everything," he said, opening the drawer of the table in the hallway to retrieve his wallet.

"Come on; you don't need much, I know the owner of the dance studio hosting the event, so I'm sure I can get us in." Vicky shrugged on her coat and led the way out the front door.

"Let's just hope that the owner of the dance studio hosting the event doesn't expect payment in the form of teaching a dance class." Lee led Vicky to his car. "Because then I'm volunteering for you."

"Nice," Vicky said, shaking her head. "Throw me under the bus, why don't you."

"Hey, all's fair in dance." Lee laughed, pulling the passenger door open for Vicky to climb in.

Lee closed the door and walked around the car. As he did, Vicky said to her coat, "If you're there, I need you to look into Judge Harkem and retired DA Joshua Armstrong for connections to the real and fake Samantha Harveys," Vicky managed to say before Lee climbed into the driver's seat of his car.

"Maybe we should've invited Pops," Lee said, backing out of his drive.

"I think you'll find that Pops is already there," Vicky told Lee. "I believe Christy and Aaron took him earlier this evening."

"Oh good, so most of my family will be there," Lee shook his head.

"I would say that all your family that is currently home will be there," Vicky informed him. "Justin, Ty, Tarryn, and all the grandkids, including your own daughter."

"Is Oliver with her?" Lee slid Vicky a sideways glance.

"I think so," Vicky said. "I believe Mya and her boyfriend are there, too. Oh, and I don't know if you heard, but Luke finally plucked up the courage to ask Tara Bright out. So, I think they'll be there."

"A dance lesson at a retirement village is the first date Luke's taking Tara on?" Lee looked pained when he looked at Vicky. "I bet that can't be going too well."

"Why wouldn't dance lessons go down well for a first date?"

Vicky asked Lee. "It's unique, and the younger generation is always looking for unique experiences these days."

"That's because they're so bored with the cyber world," Lee said. "But seriously, I don't think you get more unique than a first date at a retirement village when you're in your mid-twenties."

"Well, Luke asked her, and she said yes!" Vicky shrugged. "So, it's not like Luke just sprung it on her."

"Kind of like you did to me?" Lee grinned.

"I guess," Vicky laughed. "Who knows, you may just have fun."

"We'll see," Lee said. "It looks like quite the turnout."

The security officer at the gate to the Retirement Village waved Lee through as he knew Lee.

"You'll be surprised at how many people responded to the event. Soon we had to move to the bigger of the three halls they have here at Key West Seaside Retirement Village," Vicky told Lee. "And all by word of mouth, too."

"That's because most of the residents here know you and your dad," Lee pointed out as he pulled into an open parking space.

*D*espite his initial reservation about coming to the dance lessons event at the retirement village where Pops, Lee's grandfather lived, Lee was enjoying himself. He and Vicky had found themselves in each other's arms more than once in the past ninety minutes as he twirled her around the dance floor with the rest of the people there.

The dance instructors would take groups of people and train them in a dance routine, and then each of their groups had a turn to perform. They started out with seven groups; each group would lose three sets of dancers at a time as they were eliminated by the judges. There were snacks and beverages flowing as fun was being had by all. And Vicky had been correct when she'd told him that there was a mixed range of ages in attendance.

Lee stood watching Luke, who really had brought Dr. Tara Bright, who was slowly working her way to becoming a top surgeon, for their first date to the Retirement Village. But Vicky had been right about that, too. Lee had spoken to Tara a few minutes ago, and she was having a good time. Lee was really happy for his nephew Luke. His eyes traveled to where his niece, Mya, was dancing with her good friend Dr. Warren Pullen. Like Mya, Warren was also a child psychologist. Christy had told Lee a few days ago that Warren and Mya were starting their own practice.

Lee knew that Christy was hoping that Mya and Warren would become more than just friends. Anyone with eyes could see how Warren felt about Mya. But Mya had a boyfriend who was quite a bit older than her. He was also a doctor with an ego the size of Florida. The man was always working and hardly came to any family functions with Mya. In fact, Lee could count on his fingers the number of times Dr. Simon Wicks, Mya's boyfriend, had come to family gatherings. And the Youngs had family gatherings nearly every weekend. It was always Warren at the functions with Mya.

Lee was rooting for Warren, and maybe now that he and Mya were going to be running a business together, they might move out of the friendship zone. Like Lee hoped he and Vicky were doing. His heart did the weird jolt thing it did lately every time he saw Vicky. Her smile was forever on his mind like a portrait hanging in the background for him to see whenever she was not with him. He took a sip of his soda, and his eyes moved around the room. He felt his gut tighten when he saw Jessie being swept around the dance floor by Oliver.

Lee was still a little upset that Jessie had kept her relationship a secret for these past years. But after talking to Christy, he could understand Jessie's reasoning. It had also made Lee realize just how much his obsession with finding out what had happened to Georgia had affected Jessie. Even though he had been determined to find the truth back then, he'd always put Jessie first. But Lee now understood just how much children see and know that parents don't realize. Jessie had felt all of Lee's pain even if he'd tried his best to hide it from her.

But Jessie had been right. Had Lee known she was dating someone seriously, Lee would've uprooted his entire life in Florida to be with her in Boston. To make sure she was alright and would've become even more of a helicopter parent than he already was, especially after Jessie's ordeal with her high school boyfriend, Ian Gilbert. Lee shuddered, remembering that situation.

Ian had tried to kidnap Jessie and force her not to go to Boston. He'd not been happy when, after a year of them dating, Jessie had broken up with him because they were on separate paths. Luckily, Luke was home that day and had been asleep in the main house when he was woken by Jessie's screams. He'd rushed to the cottage to find Ian trying to drag Jessie into his car. Poor Luke had tried to stop him and had been knocked unconscious. When Ian had seen Justin running at him, he'd fumbled and dropped his keys. He had to put Jessie down in order to bend and pick them up, and that was when Justin had pounced on the kid. There was a scuffle, and Ian had pulled out a knife. Luckily Shaun Donovan had come home for lunch when he saw Ian run at Justin with a knife.

Shaun had jumped out of his car and ran to help when Justin stepped aside as Ian came at him with the knife. Ian had gotten a fright when Shaun had yelled at him. The kid had slipped on the gutter and fallen on his knife, knocking his head against the cement when he fell. The paramedics were able to stop the bleeding, but Ian had swelling on the brain and ended up in a coma. When he finally recovered, he was never the same.

Ian's parents had dragged Jessie, Justin, and Shaun to court, claiming that they had come between Ian and Jessie trying to elope. But luckily, there was more than just one witness to the scene that day as Manny Butler and his housekeeper had seen the entire thing unfold. Even though Manny didn't lift a finger to help, his housekeeper had called the police and the ambulance. Ian's parents lost the case, but Jessie started a fund for the family to help them recover medical costs that had nearly cost Ian's parents their house and everything they owned.

Lee hadn't been there when Jessie had needed him, and the Ian incident still haunted him. He knew the way he'd overreacted the night he thought Oliver was proposing to Jessie. But Lee was a father, and Jessie had been his whole world since the day he'd found out they were having a baby. He'd probably overreact a million more times in his lifetime over situations involving his daughter. Heck, Lee was like that with everyone he loved. He'd always been the older brother and he'd taken on anyone who tried to hurt a loved one. But still, Lee knew he owed Oliver an apology. Lee was waiting for the dance to finish to approach Oliver, but before he could, he saw Vicky flagging him down.

Lee noticed she was with Judge Harkem as he drew nearer to where she had just sat down.

"Ah, Lee, how are you?" Judge Harkem greeted Lee. "I hear you're leaving the DA's office to take over Donovan Law. That's a wise choice indeed."

"Thank you, Judge," Lee said, sitting down next to Vicky.

"So, what can I do for you two?" the judge asked them.

"I don't know if you heard," Vicky looked at the judge. "But Samantha Harvey quit the DA's office, and since then it's been found out that she wasn't the real Samantha Harvey."

"You don't say," the judge looked at Vicky.

"Judge, did you know she wasn't the real Samantha Harvey?" Vicky asked him.

"Am I off the record here?" The judge's shrewd eyes looked from Vicky to Lee.

"Yes," Vicky promised him. "I promise neither myself, nor Lee will repeat anything said here."

"Samantha Harvey, the real Samantha Harvey, that is," the judge said. "Was my sister's child. "She had a younger sister, Stephanie." He looked at Vicky. "Their age gap was about sixteen months apart, but they looked so much alike people would often mistake them for twins.”

“What happened to Stephanie?” Vicky asked him.

“When she three, Samantha and Stephanie were playing outside on the front lawn of my sister’s house,” the judge’s eyes clouded over. “My sister was inside making the girls their lunch when she heard Samantha scream.” A muscle ticked at the side of his jaw. “By the time my sister got to the front lawn, a car in which a man had jumped out and snatched Stephanie was driving off.”

“Oh, no!” Vicky gasped. “How horrible.”

“Luckily, my sister caught the license plate of the car,” the judge told them. “The car was tracked down to an employee of KW Research Lab. Not just any employee either. The owner of the lab’s father.”

“Did they manage to find Stephanie?” Lee’s heart was in his throat as he listened to the story.

“Yes, eventually,” the judge said. “By that time, the owner’s father had been arrested, but he refused to talk. He also told the police that his car had been stolen a few days before the incident.” The judge shook his head. “Yet he never filed a report, but they found Stephanie’s blankie in his car. She always carried around this piece of blanket. She had it with her the day she was taken.”

“I’m so sorry, Judge,” Vicky said. “Where and how was Stephanie found?”

“Two days later, an anonymous note arrived at my sister’s doorstep with where to find her daughter.” The judge’s hand shook as he ran a hand over his face. “Stephanie is a type one diabetic on insulin.”

“Oh, no!” Vicky’s eyes widened.

“When the police found Stephanie, she was going into ketone acidotic shock from a lack of food and insulin.” The judge shook his head. “The people who’d taken her had been giving her bottles of chocolate milk. They knew nothing about caring for a child, especially not a diabetic one.”

"Did Stephanie survive?" Lee asked.

"We got lucky," the judge said. "But there are plenty of other families that didn't and have suffered at the hands of these monsters."

"What do you mean?" Vicky asked, her brows furrowing together.

"Samantha may not have been much older than Stephanie, but she still had vivid memories of that day her little sister was taken," the judge ignored Vicky's question to continue his story. "Stephanie wasn't the first child this had happened to in our town, nor was she the last."

"That's awful," Vicky said. "But what has all this got to do with fake Samantha?"

"Everything," the judge said. "One of the first families to lose a child in Old Town was your grandfather and his wife." He looked at Lee.

"That's impossible," Lee said to the judge, thinking the man must be going senile. "My father lost his younger brother to a terrorist shooting while they were on vacation on some remote island that was known for unrest."

"I'm not talking about your father's younger brother; I'm talking about his older sister, Shannon Young," the judge shocked Lee by saying. "She too was around twelve or thirteen months older than your father. People often used to mistake them for twins as well because your father was a big fellow even when he was a baby, apparently."

"Judge, I think you've got the family mistaken," Vicky told him gently. "Shannon wasn't Lee's father's sister. Shannon was Lee's sister. She had a twin sister, Christy."

"I know that young lady," the judge told her scathingly. "I'm not senile just yet."

"I don't understand!" Lee's brows furrowed and he felt his mind reel. *His father had an older sister?* "How old was my father's sister when she was taken?"

"About two years old I believe," the judge said. "Only Pops

and his wife weren't as lucky as my sister was, and they never saw Shannon again."

"Do you think that's why your father named his first-born twin girl Shannon?" Vicky looked at Lee.

"I'm not sure," Lee looked at Vicky. He felt like he was buzzing from the shock of realizing he'd had an aunt who'd been kidnapped. "But if this is true, then I think so."

"Again, Judge, what has this got to do with fake Samantha?" Vicky, bless her, steered the subject away from the news of Lee's aunt.

"After the attempt on Stephanie, the news was picked up nationwide," the judge told them. "There was so much attention to the case, and although they were keeping the suspect's name out of the news, it was leaked."

"You are talking about Gordon Baxter?" Vicky asked the judge. "He was the man accused of trying to kidnap Stephanie, right?"

"See, right there is the reason these people have gotten away with what they have been doing for decades," the judge said with venom in his voice. "I know where you worked, Vicky and still you have no idea who really owns KW Labs." He looked at her. "I'm sorry, but I cannot divulge that information because I was eventually forced to take over the case on behalf of KW Labs when a few other families came forward to accuse the person."

"You ended up representing the company that tried to steal your niece?" Lee asked, dumbfounded by what the judge had just told them.

"The families were going after KW Research Lab," the judge explained. "It wasn't their fault what had happened to Stephanie; they were being dragged down by association."

"What happened to the person who'd been accused?" Vicky asked.

"He got off as there was no hard evidence linking him to the kidnapping, and no one was going to believe the word of a three-year-old." The judge pinched the bridge of his nose. "For years, the kidnappings seemed to have stopped. At least we thought they had. At least the ones that had similarities to my sister's case."

"What do you mean by similarities?" Vicky's brows creased.

"After my niece was taken, there were quite a few other families that came forward with their stories," the judge explained. "Their second eldest child had been taken, and the pattern was always the same. The kids were either the youngest twin or the youngest child that had been born eleven to thirteen months apart."

"I heard about that case," Vicky said. "The FBI was called in by a... judge," Vicky's eyes widened in realization. "It was you; you were the judge that brought the case to the FBI."

"Yes," the judge confirmed Vicky's guess. "The FBI thought it was a child trafficking ring, but the evidence trail stopped, as did the kidnappings, after Stephanie."

"Okay, so I'm assuming this somehow ties in with the real Samantha ending up in prison and getting killed?" Vicky asked.

"Yes," the judge nodded. "In 1970, a four-week-old baby was abandoned in Key West and taken in by a family. Two weeks before that, a missing child report was filed by a distraught mother in Miami." He looked directly at Lee when he said that, making warning bells go off in Lee's head. "The family that took the baby in investigated the report, but the mother was found dead two days after she'd made a nationwide appeal for her child."

"How horrible," Vicky breathed.

"It was, and her death was ruled a suicide," the judge told them. "The private clinic where the woman had gone for all her pregnancy checks and had eventually given birth claimed that the child had been stillborn and that the mother had been out of her mind with grief. Especially after having lost her husband when she was four months pregnant. He was in the air force and died in the line of duty." The judge shook his head. "The doctors at the clinic said she'd snapped and believed that she'd claimed to have heard her child cry after she'd given birth and had seen the nurses wrap the child and take it away. She was accusing the clinic of stealing her child to sell."

"Was the child stillborn?" Vicky asked.

"According to the clinic's records, the baby was," the judge told them. "But blood work on the child that had been abandoned said otherwise." He looked at Lee once again. "The story gets a little more twisted at this point."

"Why do you keep looking at...?" Lee's eyes widened. "Are you talking about...?" He swallowed, and his eyes immediately darted around the room.

"I'm not referring to anyone," the judge denied. "The abandoned baby turned out to be closely related to the family that took the child in," the judge told him. "After that, a small group of people got together, and with the help of two heroic CIA agents, started investigating the clinic where the mother had had her baby."

"What did this group, whom I'm assuming you have first-hand knowledge of," Vicky looked at the judge pointedly, "find out about the clinic?"

"Oh, many things," was all the judge would say. "Look, I've said too much, and if the both of you are wise, you'll walk away from this." He looked pointedly at Lee once again. "Your family has lost enough already, Lee," he looked at Vicky, "as has yours."

"What is that supposed to mean?" Lee asked him angrily. "And what has any of this to do with fake Samantha? Who is...?" He stopped as it dawned on him. "They looked almost exactly alike," he said and shook his head. "Stephanie was a fake Samantha."

"I cannot confirm or deny that," the judge said. "What I can tell you is this doesn't stop with the baby that was abandoned, and it's a rabbit hole neither of you wants to go down."

"I think it's a sinkhole that's been opening up at our feet for longer than we realized," Vicky said frustratedly. "Now, Judge, don't make me take you in. I'm going to ask you one last time. What is fake Samantha up to?"

"Why don't you ask her yourself, Vicky," the judge looked at her pointedly this time. "I believe she wanted to explain to you earlier." He stood up. "Now, if you excuse me, I see a lady looking for a dance partner." He stopped and looked down at Vicky. "Things aren't always as they seem, Vicky. You won't ever find all the numbers if you only scratch a few boxes."

"What does that even mean?" Lee looked up at the judge, who simply smiled down at Lee.

"Sometimes it's better to never find answers to those questions that have plagued you all these years," the judge patted Lee on the shoulder. "I'm only going to say this one more time. Walk away from this while you still can."

The judge walked off, leaving Lee and Vicky gaping at him.

Chapter Eleven

THE TROUBLE WITH DECEPTION

"We need to go speak to Pops," Lee said to Vicky.

"No, we don't." Vicky shook her head. "Not tonight anyway."

"Are you telling me that you're going to be able to go home and sleep tonight after judge Harkem dropped this bombshell on us?" Lee looked at her with narrowed eyes.

"No," Vicky said. "What I'm saying is that Pops, my father, and the rest of your family are having a good time. And after what happened to your family with the arsonist...." A thought struck her in mid-sentence, and she trailed off.

"Vicky?" Lee leaned forward and looked at her worriedly. "Are you okay?"

"Yes," Vicky said and gave him a reassuring smile. "We need to go." She stood up so abruptly that she knocked into a man, who reached out and grabbed her to steady her. "I'm so sorry," Vicky said.

"It's okay, no damage done," the man told her with a smile before giving her a slight bow and walking off. But not before Vicky felt him slip something into her pocket.

"Vicky," Lee rushed forward. "You nearly got knocked off your feet." He turned to look for the man that had knocked into her.

"It's okay, I'm fine," Vicky assured Lee. "But we really need to go."

"Where are we going?" Lee followed Vicky out the door.

"Lee, you need your coat," Vicky pointed out. She had gotten her coat before she found the judge.

"Oh, right!" Lee said and went back inside to get his coat.

Vicky waited for Lee to disappear inside before she pulled a note out of her pocket that the mysterious man who'd nearly knocked her off her feet had slipped her.

It all begins and ends with the Youngs. Speak to Roberta Davies.

Vicky's head shot up, and she looked around the grounds.

"Got it," Lee walked out of the hall with his coat. "So, where did you say we were going?"

"To get some answers," Vicky told him. "Our first stop is...." She looked at her wristwatch. *Shoot, I'm late.* "My dance studio."

"What are you hoping to find there?" Lee looked at her, confused.

"A part of this puzzle," Vicky told him. "We'd better hurry, or we might miss it."

"I have no idea what you're talking about," Lee told her, opening the car door for her. "But okay."

"Lee, is there any way you can get me in to see Roberta Davies?" Vicky asked him. "A source of mine told me that she may have some information about Samantha and KW Research Labs."

"Why would she know anything about Samantha?" Lee's eyes widened. "The fertility clinic!"

"Sorry?" Vicky frowned and looked at lee.

"Christy and Dustin used a fertility clinic when they were trying to have a second child," Lee told Vicky.

"Yes, I know that." Vicky nodded. "Oh, my word!" She looked at Lee wide-eyed. "Do you think that clinic is the same one the woman in Miami used?"

"They do operate throughout Florida," Lee pointed out. "Let me see if I can get you in to see Roberta."

"Thank you, Lee." Vicky smiled at him.

Ten minutes later, they pulled into the parking lot next to Vicky's dance studio. The lights were on in the studio, and Robin's car was in the parking lot. Vicky and Lee got out of his car and started walking towards the entrance.

"Listen, Lee," Vicky swallowed, and she looked up at him. "Before we go in there, there's something that you need to know...."

Before Vicky could tell him about Stephanie or fake Samantha as they were calling her, Lee frowned as he looked past her, and his face became cloudy with anger.

"Is that...?" Lee pointed towards the window of the studio.

Vicky froze and slowly turned around to see Stephanie quickly duck down at the window.

"Yes," Vicky closed her eyes and took a deep breath.

"What the heck is going on, Vicky?" Lee asked her through gritted teeth.

"Earlier tonight, when I was on my way to your house, I caught fake Samantha following me," Vicky told him. "Turns out that she wasn't exactly who I was led to believe she was." She shook her head. "Well, she was, and she wasn't...." She held up her hand. "That's not the point. The point is, right now, she has answers that we are both looking for."

"Both looking for?" Lee's brows furrowed. "Vicky, are you working a case?"

"I..." Vicky bit her lip.

"Vicky!" Lee's eyes clouded over. "You have been, haven't you?" He looked back at the studio. "Samantha was your case!" He breathed before giving a small mocking laugh. "Of course, that's what this has all been about." He shook his head and held up his hands.

"Lee, listen to me, please..." Vicky reasoned. "I'll explain everything to you, but first, we need to talk to fake Samantha."

"No, answer my question," Lee's eyes were filled with hurt as he stared at Vicky.

Her heart dropped, and she felt sick as she knew this was it, and he was about to find out how she'd deceived him. "Yes, I've been working one last case the agency asked me to take when they knew I was coming back to Key West."

"So, was anything over these past few days real to you?" Lee's eyes blazed down at her. "Or was I just a convenience? A tool to get you into the places you need and feed you information?"

"No!" Vicky stressed. "From the moment our eyes first met when I stepped into your dining room, I knew that I hadn't only come back home to start a new chapter in my life. I came home to find you again."

"You expect me to believe that?" Lee's frown deepened, and his eyes now shone with mistrust. "I'm going to ask you a question, and I need you to answer me honestly."

"Okay." Vicky looked at him curiously. Her heart was hammering in her chest as she could feel a hole starting to tear into it. She swallowed as she stared into his green eyes that were boring into hers.

"Jessie told me about her scheme the night at the restaurant," Lee shocked her by saying. "She swore that you had nothing to do with it or knew what she was up to." His eyes narrowed as he watched her intently. "Was she covering for you, Vicky?" A muscle started to tick in his jaw as he gritted his teeth. "Did you know what she was up to that night?"

Vicky's mouth suddenly felt dry, and her breath caught in her throat, "Yes!" she said softly.

"Yes, you were aware of what she was up to?" Lee asked her, his voice dropping dangerously low as his anger deepened. "Or yes, she was telling the truth, and you had no idea what Jessie was up to that night?"

"Yes, I knew what she was up to," Vicky swallowed the lump that was burning the back of her throat.

"So, everything that night was a lie?" Pain flashed in Lee's eyes but was quickly replaced by burning anger.

"I..." Vicky's mind was racing. "Lee, I can explain." She stepped towards him, but he raised his hand up and stepped back.

"Please, don't!" Lee shook his head. "That's all I wanted to know." He looked up at the studio. "I take it that you will be able to get home?"

"Lee!" Vicky pleaded. "Please come inside, and I will explain...."

"I'm sorry, Vicky," Lee shook his head. "I can't be here right now."

Lee turned and walked off.

"Lee!" Vicky called to him, but he ignored her and carried on walking to his car.

Vicky watched him get in and drive away, taking her heart and part of her soul with him. Tears stung her eyes as she stood staring into the dark for a few minutes after his car disappeared into the night.

"Vicky?" Robin called from the door. "Is everything okay?"

Vicky quickly wiped any stray tears away and gathered herself before turning towards Robin. "It's nothing," she said abruptly. "I take it fake Samantha or Stephanie, is still here?"

"Yes, we've been here waiting for you," Robin told her.

"Good, I have a lot of questions for both of you," Vicky's eyes narrowed into angry slits as she stalked past Robin and into the studio. "Please make sure the door is locked behind you. I think I'm still being watched."

Robin obeyed Vicky's orders. As Vicky walked towards her office, she heard Robin testing to make sure the doors were secure.

*L*ee hadn't slept much the past two nights. His mind had been too full of thoughts that led to a million questions. Questions he wasn't going to get purely by research. But Lee wasn't ready to face the one person who could answer a lot of the questions churning in his mind. It was Sunday, and for once, Lee had decided not to do any work. He needed to clear his head and try to figure out what the heck was going on right under his nose.

When Georgia had disappeared, it had opened a whole other world to Lee. For the first time after living in Key West his whole life did Lee start to see the dark underbelly that existed around him. It had been like suddenly opening his eyes and being able to see the monsters that lived in the dark shadows instead of ignorantly walking past them. Lee had been convinced that Georgia's death hadn't been an accident.

And once Lee had opened the door to the shadow world, he had found it hard to close it again. Even when he had been able to push it aside, Lee was very aware of what lurked around him. That was another reason he'd become even more protective of his daughter and family. Lee was terrified of losing anyone else to what he'd come to know as the shadow world—the seedy parts of life that operated behind the scenes, and anyone who crossed the line or interfered with it turned up missing or dead.

Lee pulled on a t-shirt as he walked out of his room towards the kitchen. He could smell a pot of fresh coffee brewing and knew he was about to be accosted by a member of his family as he had been each morning since the night of his date with Vicky, which was three nights ago. He frowned as he corrected his earlier thoughts. He'd actually not gotten much sleep in three nights, not two. His brain was in such a state that he was losing days now. Lee braced himself for whoever he was about to find in his kitchen.

Today he found Jessie sitting at the kitchen counter on one of the stools. She was sipping a cup of coffee with a big bowl of cereal in front of her.

"Good morning, sweetheart," Lee said, walking into the kitchen. "I see you drew the short straw today."

"Nope," Jessie shook her head. "I told your siblings to lay off of you for the day, and I came here to be with my dad because I've missed our morning breakfasts together."

"That's nice of you." Lee opened the fridge and took out the milk. "I've missed you too." He put two slices of bread in the toaster and poured himself a cup of coffee. "But now, do you want to tell me why you're really here?"

"Would you believe that I ran out of cereal in the pool house?" Jessie grinned at him.

"If the cupboards in your apartment in Boston were anything to go on," Lee said. "Yes, I would believe you ran out of cereal. But I don't believe that's the only reason you're here."

"You're right," Jessie told him. "I'm here because Oliver and I want you and his mother to come to dinner with us tonight."

"Why?" Lee stopped and leaned on the counter in front of Jessie.

"Can't we just want to have a nice dinner with our parents?" Jessie asked innocently.

"Honey," Lee sighed. "What's going on?"

"If you want to know that, then you have to go to dinner with us tonight." She gave him a smug smile.

"Fine," Lee relented. "Message me the restaurant and the time."

"Great!" Jessie clapped excitedly. "Now, for the other reason, I'm here."

"Ah..." Lee nodded. "There it is!"

"Are you ever going to tell me what happened between you and Aunt Vicky?" Jessie asked.

"Nothing." Lee shrugged and took a sip of his coffee. "Are you going to tell me what the dinner with you, Oliver, and his mother is all about?"

"No." Jessie shook her head. "Then you won't come to the dinner."

"Okay, so we're at an impasse then." Lee grinned and took another sip of his coffee. "How about information for information?"

"No," Jessie declined his offer. "I'll just go ask Aunt Vicky."

"Fine," Lee said. "I'll just go and have a word with Oliver." He raised his eyebrows and gave her a smug smile. "I think he and I have become great friends since dinner last night."

"You wouldn't dare!" Jessie's eyes narrowed.

"Oh, is that a challenge?" Lee asked.

"No, that wasn't a challenge," Jessie said.

"Well, I think you threw down the gauntlet, and I accept the challenge," Lee told her. "Let's see who can get the information they are looking for the fastest."

"I know what you're doing," Jessie told him, sitting back and folding her arms in front of her. "I'm not a child anymore. I won't fall for reverse-reverse manipulation tactics."

"I'll make you a deal," Lee said. "You leave mine and Vicky's personal lives alone, and I'll come willingly to this dinner."

"Okay," Jessie accepted. "It's a deal." She held out her hand. "Shake on it?"

"Of course," Lee shook his hand. "My word and handshake is my promise."

"Glad to hear that," Jessie grinned mischievously. "That was easy!"

And just like Lee realized he'd been played by the outstanding intelligent mind of his beautiful daughter.

"Why you little manipulator..." Lee eyed her suspiciously. "You played me." He shook his head. "You already spoke to Vicky, didn't you?"

"I'll never tell," Jessie told him, looking smugger by the minute. "But your handshake is your word and your bond. So, I've just sent you the time and restaurant. Don't be late."

Jessie finished off her cereal and her coffee.

"Are you looking forward to starting your new job tomorrow?" Lee changed the subject.

"I am," Jessie said. "Can you borrow Aunt Christy's minivan tomorrow, please?"

"Is that your way of asking me if you can use my car to go to work?" Lee looked at her questioningly.

"Dad, please can you borrow Aunt Christy's car tomorrow so I can borrow your cool SUV to go to my first day of work?"

Jessie smiled at him sweetly. "Oliver's car hasn't arrived yet, so I'm giving him a lift to work, and even when his car does arrive, I want to take my own."

"That's not being very environmentally friendly," Lee pointed out. "For a scientist, that's really irresponsible, honey."

"You drive to work on your own every day," Jessie pointed out. "If you are going to point a finger, make sure you don't have the other three pointing back at you. Isn't that what grandma used to say?" She grinned.

"You are in top form this morning," Lee observed. "What are you up to today?"

"Mya and I are going shopping for our house," Jessie told him. "Then we are going to go to Ocean Cafe for lunch."

"Nice," Lee said and finished off his coffee.

"What are you doing today?" Jessie asked him.

"I'm going to take the day off from the outside world," Lee told her. "I'm going to read a newspaper, go for a walk, and then maybe even take a nap sometime during the day."

"Wow!" Jessie said sarcastically. "A whole day of exhilaration."

"Correct!" Lee grinned. "If you weren't dragging me out to dinner tonight, we could've had our traditional junk food Sunday movie night."

"Are you trying to coerce me to cancel our dinner plans?" Jessie raised her eyebrows.

"Your dinner plans," Lee reminded her. "I'm just the poor guy that got suckered into having to be there."

"I promise it's not going to be painful." Jessie laughed at the look on her father's face. "I might be swayed out of dinner if you bought me a car for Christmas."

"What happened to the car you had in Boston?" Lee asked her.

"I sold it," Jessie reminded him. "Remember, you told me to invest the money I got from the sale and promised to buy me another one when I got back to Key West."

"No, I promised to help you buy one when you got to Key West," Lee pointed out. "Meaning, you had to take responsibility for part of the car payment. Remember, we agreed that as soon as you started to work, I would ease back on being your ATM."

"I know," Jessie assured him. "But we agreed when I was working and in a position to do so."

"I'm not going to win with you anytime soon, am I?" Lee sighed. "How about this?" he bargained. "I'll let you use the sedan—it needs to be driven more anyway—until we can get you a new car."

"Really?" Jessie's eyes lit up. "You'll let me use the sedan?"

"I will," Lee nodded. "But there are rules, and we have to get you insured first."

"Thank you, Dad!" Jessie sprung off her chair to give him a hug. "But because I'm already insured to drive the SUV, I can borrow that tomorrow, right?"

"Fine," Lee said. "I have to put new tires on the sedan as well. I'll do that during the week, and then you can take it."

"You are the best dad ever," Jessie praised him. "I best be going. Mya and I are leaving soon."

"Enjoy your day, sweetheart," Lee said, giving her a hug. "Please be careful."

"I always am," Jessie assured him, giving him a wave before walking out of the back door to go through their backyard to the pool house.

Lee stood watching her go before remembering he'd put toast on. He turned to see that it had popped out a little while ago because the toast was cool. He sighed and pulled it out of the toaster. This is what his life felt like right now. Cold toast that nothing melted on. Instead, it just congealed on the top of it in a gooey mess. Lee took a bite of his cold toast and walked through to the living room, where he flopped onto the couch.

While he ate his toast, his eyes fell on his notebook. Lee leaned forward and picked it up, opening it to what he'd written down the night before after his dinner guests had left. Lee pulled out a piece of paper he'd found on the passenger seat that must've fallen out of Vicky's pocket the night she'd come to supper, and they'd gone to the function as the retirement village.

It all begins and ends with the Youngs. Speak to Roberta Davies.

Lee didn't think this message was for him. Someone must've slipped it to Vicky. He'd been avoiding thinking about that night because he still felt like he'd been a few rounds with a champion fighter. Only his soul had been the boxing ring and his heart the target. An image of Vicky standing up and a man knocking into her flashed through his mind. The man turned to her and said something when Vicky had apologized. At the time, Lee hadn't thought anything of it, but now he thought that perhaps the man had slipped this note into her pocket.

Lee frowned. He'd only caught a glimpse of the man, but there'd been something familiar about him. Lee looked at the message. This must've been why Vicky wanted to see Roberta. Lee felt a twinge of guilt zip through him at how he'd been so quick to judge Vicky. Maybe Jessie wasn't just lying to try and mend the fences between him and Vicky, and it was Jessie's plan to break Lee and Samantha up.

Lee gave himself a mental shake. No, Vicky had admitted that she knew about the plan to break up his relationship. He pinched the bridge of his nose as he tried to squash out the little niggling voice at the back of his mind. The voice was telling him he hadn't given Vicky a fair chance to explain her side of the story. Lee had been so afraid of what he was feeling for Vicky that he'd jumped at any excuse to walk away before she could leave him.

Lee knew he'd stayed with fake Samantha for so long because the relationship was comfortable. While Lee had cared for the woman he'd thought Samantha was, he wasn't in love with her. Fake Samantha had become his shield against his family and friends that had been trying to set him up for years. Lee had known that deep down, and it hadn't been a problem because it wasn't until the last six weeks of their relationship that Samantha started pushing for it to go to the next level.

But when Lee had seen Vicky again, he'd known that his

relationship with Samantha was over. Lee looked at the ring box on the table. He had to take it back tomorrow. Lee had been such a fool. He knew now why he suddenly felt the need to get engaged. So, he could cower behind his Samantha shield and deny his feelings for Vicky. Lee sighed. He'd really made a mess of everything. Lee knew he needed to fix his relationship with Vicky, but right now, he had other matters swirling in his head. Like the story that Judge Harken had told them about the child that had been abandoned. Lee had already started looking into the clinic where the child's mother had given birth.

Lee had already confirmed that the clinic where the abandoned child's mother had given birth did specialize in infertility treatments. They were also the same chain of clinics that Lee's sister Christy and her late husband Dustin had gone to in Key West when they were trying to have a second child. Christy and Dustin had paid a fortune for the treatments, which hadn't worked. It was six months later, when Christy and Dustin took a second honeymoon, that Christy had become pregnant the more natural way.

But another person had used that same clinic that Dustin and Christy had. Lee looked down at the message. Roberta Davies, the arsonist who'd been in love with Christy's late husband, had also used the clinic. She was also the woman that Dustin had rescued from the burning building that had taken his life. Roberta Davies had a daughter who Christy recently found out had been Dustin's child. Dustin hadn't had an affair with Roberta. Roberta had allegedly broken into the fertility clinic that Christy and Dustin had used. That was how Roberta had managed to have Dustin's child.

When Christy had found out about what Roberta had done, no one thought to question whether or not the clinic's story about the break-in checked out. So, Lee had started to do some digging into the clinic. He found that the clinic had been sued on numerous occasions for *losing* their customers' precious samples they had entrusted with the clinic. How did a clinic lose samples? Were they not storing them correctly, and the samples were no longer viable?

Lee rubbed his chin as his mind turned over the various possibilities. One glaringly obvious one would be that the clinic was using samples their customers were paying for them to store to other customers that came to them for help. The clinic did have an over-average higher success rate than a lot of the other top clinics. It was also a clinic where parents had a one-stop-shop for all their new family needs, from pregnancy care through to birth. They had a full house of pediatric doctors for their child's care. They even had their own range of vitamins and supplements for parents wanting to start a family, mothers-to-be, and postnatal care. The clinic also offered what they called different grading care. This allowed the clinic to offer their high-end services to any family, no matter their income. Lee's eyes narrowed when he looked at the pamphlet he'd picked up for the clinic that was located in Key West. The clinic even had a branch that helped those who couldn't afford health care.

Lee was going to pay a visit to both clinics located in Key West during the next week. Jessie had agreed to help him. Oliver and Jessie were going to find out how they could help them start their new family. Lee shuddered. He really didn't like to think of Jessie so grown up that she was ready to get married and start a family of her own. But Lee knew it was inevitable, and as much as he wanted to dislike Oliver, Lee couldn't find a thing wrong with him. Although, he had asked his cousin, Tarryn, to quietly find out what she could about Oliver and his family.

Tarryn had been reluctant, but she'd relented and said she would do it, but if they were caught, this would all come down on Lee's head. He'd agreed to those terms. But after the Ian incident…. Lee shuddered again. He would risk his daughter's fury and the possibility that she would never speak to him again to ensure she was safe. Lee looked at the message again. There was another reason he needed to look into the clinics. The story Judge Harkem had told Lee and Vicky about the abandoned baby had rung too close to home, and Lee needed to find out the truth. He planned to start by asking his grandfather if his first child had been a daughter that had gone missing when she was roughly two years old.

Lee needed to know what the message meant about it all starting and ending with the Youngs. Did the message mean that his family had something to do with the kidnappings? Why would Pops have his own daughter kidnapped? Nothing made much sense right now, and Lee needed to get his life to fall back neatly into place. How could he ever possibly think of starting anything with Vicky when his life was falling to pieces? Lee couldn't pull her into whatever dark rabbit hole this was all leading to. Lee got up and walked through to go have a shower with the little voice in his head calling him a coward. He also knew he needed Vicky's help with investigating.

Chapter Twelve

A RESTRICTED AREA

"Vicky!" Justin greeted her. "Where are you off to so bright and early?"

"Hello, Justin," Vicky greeted him with a warm smile, although his posture said he wasn't here for a friendly chat. "What brings you to my house so early?"

"Oh, I was just going for a walk," Justin told her.

"Really?" Vicky leaned against the side of her car and folded her arms.

"Anything interesting going on with you lately?" Justin asked.

"Nope!" Vicky shook her head. "Just the usual. Getting the dance studio ready for the grand reopening in a week's time."

"I see your father still comes home every day for lunch," Justin said casually. But Vicky knew there was more behind his statement.

"Yes," Vicky confirmed. "I guess old habits never die."

"You and your father were supposed to come over for dinner the other night," Justin looked at her questioningly. "Christy said your father wasn't feeling well, so you canceled. I hope he's okay?"

"Dad just had a bit of a stomach upset," Vicky told him. "You know how it is. The older we get, the more of the foods we once loved we can't really eat anymore."

"Tell me about it," Justin laughed. "I've had to go on a gluten-free diet."

"Luckily, most places cater for people who have a gluten intolerance," Vicky said. She needed to go have a talk with an old friend, so she had to get him to leave. "Okay, Justin, what is this really about?"

"Can't a neighbor just stop by and be sociable anymore?" Justin tried to look offended by her affront.

"Not when that neighbor is you," Vicky told him honestly. "So out with it!"

"Fine!" Justin said. "It's come to my attention that the FBI had taken quite an interest in the disappearance of Samantha Harvey and my brother."

"I don't know anything about that," Vicky lied. "Well, I know what Christy and Lee have told me."

"Which is probably about the same as what Lee had told me," Justin said. "Look, I know you're semi-retired, but can you please find out if they are also investigating Lee?" His eyes met and held Vicky's. She could see the worry shining in their depths. "You know what Lee went through with Georgia's disappearance, and I just don't want any surprises thrown at us."

"Are you asking me to find out for you?" Vicky's brows drew together.

"Don't tell me you haven't thought about it or already started looking into it," Justin looked at her accusingly. "Because I've known you your whole life, and I know that's what you do for the people you love."

"That's true," Vicky admitted. "But Justin, you know I can't discuss official FBI business with you."

"But you can tell a concerned brother if he has anything to be concerned about," Justin pointed out. "I also know that you're not the agent investigating the case and that the agent that is..." He gave her a smug smile.

"Nice!" Vicky smiled. "Fine, I'll let you know what I can when I have anything to tell you."

"Is that a roundabout way of telling me you're not really

going to tell me anything of importance?" Justin was way sharper than Vicky gave him credit for.

Justin had always been the jock of the family. But Vicky knew he was a secret nerd.

"No," Vicky sighed. "I promise, Justin, as soon as I know what's going on, I'll let you know."

"Thank you, Vicky," Justin smiled. "Oh, and was that Jack I saw passing you something the other night at the dance?"

"Jack?" Vicky asked, confused. "I don't know any...."

Images of the night she was supposed to have dinner with Lee and had ended up ending their relationship before it began flashed through her mind. Vicky had shot up out of her chair and knocked into a giant wall of a man. But it wasn't her that had knocked into him. The man had deliberately collided with her. Vicky had been so distracted with the information Judge Harkem had given them that she hadn't paid much attention to what the man looked like. Well, not until she'd looked in her pocket. But by the time she'd gone to find him, he'd been long gone. But apparently, Justin had gotten a good enough look at the man to identify him. And that wasn't good.

"Come on, Vicky, share!" Justin cocked his head.

"I only pieced it together now," Vicky admitted. At least part of that was true. "I was so distracted after Judge Harkem told us a story about a mother in Miami."

"Oh?" Justin's brows drew together. "Why would Judge Harken tell you and Lee a story about a mother in Miami?"

"Lee and I were talking with him about fake Samantha," Vicky explained.

"I like that." Justin laughed. "Fake Samantha."

"We wondered why fake Samantha would use Samantha Harvey's name," Vicky told Justin. "Do you know who Samantha Harvey is?"

"Yes, they called her the black widow," Justin said. "Her first husband of two years died under mysterious circumstances in 1999."

"Correct," Vicky confirmed. "She married again three years

later, and once again, her husband died under mysterious circumstances."

"But it wasn't until her fiancé was killed quite brutally that they started digging into her previous marriages," Justin said.

"Correct," Vicky nodded. "Lee and I were wondering how the DA's office would hire Samantha Harvey, especially when the woman had died several years ago in prison."

"So, you went to find who had hired her and slipped her in through the back door," Justin guessed.

"We found our connection," Vicky told Justin.

"Judge Harkem?" Justin's brows drew together as he looked at Vicky in disbelief.

"Yes," Vicky confirmed. "Turns out that dear Judge Harkem was, in fact, Samantha Harvey's uncle."

"Okay!" Justin held up his hands. "Why would he risk that?"

"He was retiring," Vicky pointed out. "He told us in a roundabout way why he'd planted fake Samantha in the DA's office."

"And that was?" Justin looked at Vicky expectantly. "To incriminate himself and go out with a bang?"

"That stifled me for the past two days as well." Vicky laughed at Justin's suggestion. "But then it clicked, and I did some digging and found out that my assumptions were correct."

"Okay, that's very cryptic, Vicky," Justin said, throwing up his hands in frustration. "You have to give me more here."

"I'm not one hundred percent sure, so I shouldn't have said my assumptions were correct," Vicky corrected her previous statement. "But I think he put Samantha where he did deliberately."

"Okay!" Justin looked a little confused. "Why would a man with his impeccable record want to blow up years of a career he'd fought his way to build up?" He shook his head. "You know his roots, right?"

"I do, now," Vicky nodded. "I think it was because of a major client of his."

"He wanted to expose the client without breaking attorney-client privileges," Justin said. "Getting Samantha Harvey into a

DA's office would eventually draw someone's attention." He looked at Vicky accusingly. "Which it did, and that's why you're really here."

"No, that is not the only reason I'm here," Vicky corrected Justin. "I am retired, but I was asked to take one last case because of where I was moving to."

"And because you wanted something in return?" Justin's shrewd eyes picked up on Vicky's slight hesitation when she'd told him the case wasn't the only reason she was back in Key West.

"No," Vicky denied. "I just wanted to be able to retire in peace."

"That's a fair trade," Justin agreed. "Well, I'd better be going. I have a whole day of lazing around to do."

"I see you haven't changed your usual Sunday routine since you were a boy." Vicky shook her head at him.

"Why mess with what works?" Justin shrugged. He looked down at her shoes. "Cool hiking boots."

"Oh, yes," Vicky looked down at her feet. "They are so comfortable."

"So, you're still into all the extreme sports you and Christy liked to do so much," Justin noted.

"I wouldn't call hiking an extreme sport," Vicky said.

"I guess that depends on where you're hiking." Justin gave her a sly smile. "Well, gotta run... lots of doing nothing to be done. Please keep me updated."

"Of course," Vicky said before saying goodbye, getting in her car and pulling off.

*V*icky drove out of town and turned into a restricted area that was only accessible to Florida Fish and Wildlife Conservation staff members. She parked her car where it couldn't be seen. Vicky pulled a backpack and hat from her trunk. She pulled a stick of insect repellent from her bag and dabbed it all over her skin before pulling her jacket and hat on. Vicky shoved the bottle bag in her backpack and shrugged the backpack over both of her shoulders before setting off into the large trees that hid treasures deeper within the forest.

Vicky loved this walk, although she wouldn't want to do it at night. It was bad enough that she could feel human eyes watching her every move these days. She wouldn't want to add the critters' eyes watching her. Vicky shuddered. Not many people knew about this hidden mangrove swamp with its thick canopy of trees that opened out in the most beautiful and peaceful body of water. But it was a hotbed for mosquitoes, especially in the summer. Vicky walked through the long line of trees on the well walked footpath until she stepped through an opening, and the world around her brightened once again.

The water next to Vicky sparkled as it meandered around the trunks of all the trees that looked like they were holding up their branches while they cooled off in the water. Vicky smiled to herself as she imagined the foliage chatting about the heat and then all stopping to stare at the human invading their space. Vicky walked over the bridge that spanned the swamp and sloshed through some wetland patches until she came to another clearing. She looked up at the timber structure towering over her propped up by thick wooden beams.

"You know you shouldn't be here!" A deep voice said from behind her.

Vicky had known he was there and had probably been following her since she'd pulled into the reserve.

"You knew I'd only come here if I really had to," Vicky said.

"Have you come to relieve me of my babysitting duty?" he asked her.

"Not quite yet," Vicky said, still facing forward and not looking at him. "But you really need to put a leash on your houseguest."

"I've noticed he's been missing a lot lately," the man said.

"Did you know he's been using your identity to access records?" Vicky asked him.

"I'm going to kill him!" the man hissed. "Is that why you're here?"

"No, your houseguest got sloppy and was seen by a U.S. Marshal," Vicky told him.

"Do you want me to take care of him?" he asked her.

"No," Vicky shook her head, turned around, and smiled. "But you might want to reign him in and keep a closer eye on him."

"I was talking about the U.S. Marshal," he said.

"No!" Vicky's brows furrowed together. "Leave him be. I can deal with him."

"Really?" he asked her, not looking convinced. "Because you know he's been following you, right?"

"What?" Vicky looked taken aback. "No way; why would he be following me?"

"I don't know." The man looked at her before saying, "Why don't we ask him." He used his chin to point behind her.

Vicky spun around and froze. "Justin, what the blazes are you...?" her voice trailed off when she saw the woman trailing behind him and moaning every step of the way.

"I told you if you're going to drag me into a swamp, I need mosquito repellent." The woman was half Justin's height, but Vicky bet she could give Justin a good run for his money if she really wanted to. She stopped, and her eyes widened when she saw Vicky. "Uh..." She looked around awkwardly like she was looking for an escape route before looking at Vicky again. "Hey, Vicky."

Vicky didn't say anything; she just stared at the woman and shook her head in disgust.

"I was wondering where you were going, all dressed for a hike," Justin explained. "While I was getting in my car to follow you, imagine my surprise when I found Tilly sneaking around my house."

"Another one of your strays!" He shook his head in disgust. "Now, can I get rid of the U.S. Marshal?" He looked around pointedly. "I can throw him in the swamp and let the ecosystem take care of him."

"I like the new dance studio, Vicky," Justin stopped a few feet in front of her. "This place is amazing."

"It is beautiful," the five-foot-four woman said softly and started to squirm beneath Vicky's angry glare.

"Care to explain?" Justin grabbed the woman and pushed her forward. "Why were you hiding another one of my relations?"

"Don't you have ears?" Vicky glared at the woman Justin called Tilly. "I told you to lie low during the day and especially on weekends."

"I just wanted to see Justin," Tilly said softly. "I'm sorry, but I miss my family so much."

"I can take care of them both," the man assured her.

"No!" Vicky hissed at him, not to be sure if he meant it or not, but she wasn't leaving it to chance. "Looks like you're getting another houseguest after all."

"I don't have room," he said immediately.

"You have a six-bedroom house!" Vicky pointed out.

"I need a gym and a study." He folded his arms across his chest and stood his ground.

"That still leaves you with three free bedrooms," Vicky told him.

"I need those too." He shrugged. "Look, it's bad enough you got me babysitting the brick wall. I'm not taking care of Tiny Tilly as well." He glared at Vicky. "And look how both of them listen. They clearly had no regard for their own lives, let alone the danger they are dragging everyone around them into when they don't listen." He shook his head. "No! I'm sorry, but I won't do it."

"Hey," the woman said angrily. "You know we can hear you."

"See, and she's nosy too," he pointed out. "You know how I feel about reporters. Especially investigative ones."

"I don't want to stay here either, buddy," Tilly assured him. "Vicky, please. I promise I will not leave the basement ever again."

"Whoa!" Justin held up his hands. "No one is staying anywhere. I should take all four of you in."

"Unless you're including yourself in this equation, Justin, there are only three of us," Tilly pointed out to Justin.

"I'm talking about him," Justin pointed behind Vicky, who turned to see the man Vicky referred to as the houseguest standing quietly behind them. "How are you doing, Jack?"

"Justin," Jack, who was six-foot-five, usually topped most men in a room, stepped next to Vicky protectively.

"Jack!" Tilly's face lit up with a mixture of surprise and relief. She nearly pushed Justin over the bridge and into the swamp as she rushed past him towards Jack.

Jack bent down and lifted her into his arms for a bear hug. "Hey, kiddo," he said.

"I thought you were dead!" Tilly punched Jack on a bulging bicep. "Why did you do that to me?" She hit him again angrily, and tears sprung to her eyes while she patted the solid chest that was straining against his t-shirt. "I saw the bullet lodged in your chest... there was so much blood."

Jack put Tilly down and smiled gently down at her. "Vicky saved me," he told Tilly softly. "I owe her my life and that of my wife, my son, and you."

"You went back?" Tilly looked at Vicky wide-eyed. "Then who was on the chopper with us?"

"You can thank your chopper pilot for that," Vicky reached behind their host's back and gave it a pat. "Tilly, I'd like you to meet Garry."

"Is that your real name?" Tilly's eyes narrowed as her eyes traveled over the scar on Garry's face. "What happened to your face?"

"Tilly!" Jack hissed. "That's rude."

"It's okay," Garry said. "Let's just say I had a fight with a giant spider that was trying to kill me."

"What happened to the spider?" Tilly asked.

"I think that's enough trivia for today!" Vicky stopped Tilly before she managed to dig any deeper. "The less you know about Garry, the better."

"Is that because Special Agent Garry is one of the most

wanted people in the U.S. at the moment?" Justin gave Garry a smug smile.

"You must have old information," Garry told Justin coolly without so much as batting an eyelid. "All charges against me were dropped."

"Then why are you living out here harboring other wanted criminals?" Justin looked directly at Jack.

"I have no idea what you're talking about," Garry denied all knowledge of Jack's criminal history. "Who I have visiting me is none of anyone's business." His eyes warred with Justin's, and a slow smile spread across his lips. Garry held Justin's glare as he said to Vicky. "Fine, Tiny Tilly can stay here."

"Oh, no!" Justin walked up to Tilly and pulled her away from the three of them. "There is no way I'll let my baby sister stay here and get her in even more trouble than she's already in."

"Justin, you know Tilly has to stay hidden," Vicky reasoned with him. "My father was hiding her until I found out, and I've been looking for another safe place for her to hide."

"She can't stay at your place, Justin," Jack tried to reason with Justin.

"Seriously, V," Garry said softly. "No one will even know if I dump his body in the swamp."

"Hey!" Tilly spun around and advanced and Garry, who was only a foot shorter than Jack. "What is your problem?" Her green eyes blazed with anger. "We don't want to be in your swamp any more than you want us here."

"Well, then leave," Garry wasn't fazed by Tilly's anger. "I'm not stopping you."

"Too bad!" Tilly hissed. "Because you know what? This mosquito-infested hell hole is starting to grow on me. I think I'll stay after all." She folded her arms in front of her and stood her ground.

"Trust me, Tiny Tilly, you won't last two days out here without your princess comforts," Garry's cool eyes held hers without so much as flinching. "You'll soon be crying for your big brother to come and get you." His eyes looked up and met

Justin's. "And if he ever sets foot in my swamp again, I'll be introducing him to some hungry fish."

"Is that a threat?" Justin started to step forward. But Tilly put out her hand and stopped him.

"Are you threatening my brother?" Tilly spat. "Oh... you're going to pay for that." She raised an eyebrow at him.

"What are you going to do, Tiny Tilly?" Garry laughed. "Bore me to death?"

"That's enough!" Vicky's voice cracked through the air like a whip, making everyone stand to attention. "What is this? Preschool?' She looked at the three of them. "In case any of you have forgotten, you all have a huge target on your backs."

"I don't," Justin said.

"Actually, Justin, there's more to the story that Judge Harkem told me," Vicky said. "And I think your family is at the center of whatever is going on."

Vicky caught Jack and Tilly exchanging a look, and her eyes narrowed. "What was that?" She pointed to the two of them.

"What was what?" Tilly asked Vicky innocently.

"That look you and Jack shared." Vicky's eyes narrowed dangerously. "What are you keeping from me?"

Tilly's eyes slid nervously towards Justin. "Nothing!" she said.

"Jack!" Vicky glared at him, and he just shrugged. "Fine." She shrugged and turned to Garry, stepping forward to whisper something to him. Garry nodded and looked at Jack and Tilly.

"What's going on?" Tilly asked Vicky.

"They're trying to scare you, kiddo," Jack told her, standing protectively by her side.

"Justin, we need to leave," Vicky told him.

"Oh, no!" Justin said stubbornly. "Do you really think I'm going to leave my sister here with America's most wanted?"

"I told you I'm not wanted," Garry said through clenched teeth.

"Anymore..." Justin provoked him. "You're not wanted anymore!"

"Justin..." Vicky warned him. "I promise you M... Tilly's in safe hands. Besides, the mountain won't let anything happen to her. In case you hadn't noticed, Jack's very protective over Tilly."

"Justin," Jack walked up to him. "I know things are messy and out of hand right now. But I promise you that I didn't kill those people."

"He didn't!" Tilly stepped up next to Jack. "I was there. But..." She glanced at Vicky.

"But..." Vicky's eyes narrowed.

"My cousin and Jack's sister wouldn't let me clear Jack's name," Tilly told them.

"Why?" Justin asked. "Why would they implicate Jack if he was innocent?"

"I can't tell you that," Tilly said. "And please don't try to make me."

"Why didn't you come forward and say anything?" Justin looked at Jack.

Vicky noticed Jack closed his eyes and took a deep breath.

"Jack, don't!" Vicky warned him. "Remember the less people who know...."

"It's okay, Vicky," Jack smiled at her. "I trust Justin."

"I don't," Garry said. "I think this is a very bad idea, and we should not let the U.S. Marshal leave this swamp. He could risk everything we're trying to do."

"You leave my brother alone!" Tilly whirled around and glared at Garry. "Why do men always underestimate women? Especially when they're short like me?"

"Maybe because you're like a teeny little annoying flea?" Garry said.

"Think on this for a minute," Tilly's eyes narrowed to angry slits. "I've traveled all over the world and studied so many cultures that you didn't even know existed. I know more than one hundred ways to kill someone without ever touching them." She gave him an evil grin. "You may be a lot bigger and meaner than me, but you've still got to eat, sleep, and drink sometime."

"Bring it!" Garry challenged. "Trust me, Tiny Tilly, more dangerous women than you have tried to kill me."

"Okay, that's it!" Justin stepped forward, but before he moved another step, Vicky stopped him.

"Calm down," Vicky told him. "We're going to go home now. On the way, we'll stop at the ice cream shack, and I will tell you everything you want to know. But you have to forget you ever came here, or you are putting a lot more lives than yours in danger. Including your little sister's."

"I promise you, Justin," Jack told him. "I won't let anything happen to Tilly."

"And I must just trust you?" Justin's brows furrowed. "You were accused of murdering three people and putting a twelve-year-old boy in a coma."

"To be fair, the kid was military trained and was about to kill Jack's son," Tilly stood up for Jack. "And it wasn't J..." she started to say but stopped herself. Her eyes were wide, and she put her hand up to her mouth.

"You still want to leave her here?" Garry shook his head in disgust. "Vicky, what about...."

"It's okay," Vicky assured Garry. "Jack, maybe you should tell Justin."

"The reason I never came forward is because the knife that killed those three people and put the kid in a coma..." Jack swallowed, looked down, and took a deep breath. "Let's just say it didn't belong to me. It belonged to someone close to me."

"I saw that person and someone close to us washing blood off their hands and then going to burn their clothes," Tilly finished for Jack. "I also saw the older of the two take the knife and put it into Jack's belongings after smearing the clothes he had on the previous day with the bloodied knife."

"Wait!" Justin looked at them in disbelief. "Are you implicating who I think you're implicating?" he asked.

"When Tilly tried to come forward, she was threatened," Vicky continued the story.

"By one of the two who allegedly killed those people in cold blood?" Justin looked like he couldn't believe what he was hearing.

"No," Tilly shook her. "By forces much worse."

"Who?" Justin asked.

"A CIA agent," Tilly told him. "They told me that if I came forward, they would implicate me with Jack, and I would never see my family again."

"Jack was captured, and that's when Tilly came to me for help," Vicky explained to Justin.

"That was nearly seven years ago." Justin's eyes widened. "Right around the time, we all lost contact with you."

"Yes," Tilly nodded. "I had to go into hiding because the CIA was hunting me down."

"Or a CIA agent was hunting her down," Jack said. "Vicky, Garry, and Tilly, who I believe stowed away with them, and two other agents saved me when I was being transported."

"That was you?" Justin stared at Vicky in astonishment.

"No," Vicky shook her head. "It was a group of people who were sick of seeing people abuse their positions to cover up their crimes and then pin them on innocent people."

"Fair enough," Justin understood. "This is a lot to take in," he said. "I need time to process all this."

"We need to leave," Vicky looked at Justin. "But, we need your word that you will not mention anything about any of this. Not even to *any* of your family."

"I still have a lot of questions," Justin looked at all of them.

"I'll answer them," Vicky promised him. "But we really need to leave now."

"I'll be fine," Tilly assured Justin.

"Jack, I swear if anything happens to my little sister...." Justin threatened him, and his eyes slid towards Garry warningly.

"I understand," Jack nodded.

Vicky managed to drag Justin away after he shot a few more warnings at Garry.

"Trust me, Garry won't harm a hair on their heads," Vicky told Justin. "They are in the safest hands with him."

"Why do you trust that man?" Justin asked her.

"That man is the *only* person I trust right now," Vicky told him. "Justin, you know you can walk away from this right now."

"No," Justin shook his head. "If my family is in the middle of this, then no." He shook his head emphatically. "I'm in, whatever you need."

"Thank you," Vicky sighed in relief. "Because I do need two huge favors."

"Try me," Justin shrugged.

Justin asked Vicky a few more questions about the mission that had implicated Jack and Tilly by association. Vicky told him what he wanted to know.

"Meet me at the ice cream shack," Vicky told Justin. "There's something you need to see."

Justin nodded and climbed into his SUV. Vicky pulled out of the restricted area and headed towards the designated meeting place.

INTERVIEW WITH A SERIAL ARSONIST

"I got you fifteen minutes," Justin told Vicky. "Let's go."

"Thanks," Vicky walked through to the interview room.

Roberta Davies was already there waiting for them.

"Another Young," Roberta said, looking at Justin. "It must be my lucky day." She turned her head to look at Vicky. "And you're the best friend, Vicky, is it?"

"Roberta, do you know why we're here?" Vicky asked her.

"You want to talk about the fires," Roberta rolled her eyes. "How many times do I have to go over and over this?"

"We're not here about the fires, Roberta," Vicky pointed to the chairs in front of Roberta. "Do you mind if we sit down?"

"Sure," Roberta looked shocked that Vicky had asked permission to sit down. "What do you want to talk about?"

"Roberta, before we start, can I say how deeply sorry I am for the loss of your daughter," Vicky gave her a small smile. "I know it's not the exact same thing. But I lost my baby daughter when she was two months old." She bit her lip. "I named her Angel, and she spent the two months of her life in an incubator because she was born at seven months."

"I'm sorry," Roberta's eyes filled with compassion as she stared at Vicky. "It doesn't matter if we carried them for a few hours in our belly or had them in our lives until they were grown. A parent should never outlive their child. Any loss of a child resonates at the same frequency of pain no matter how long they've been in a parent's life for."

"Yes," Vicky agreed, her eyes misting over. "Angel had been my third pregnancy. But the only one I was able to carry until giving birth."

"I can understand that," Roberta swallowed. "It took me three attempts to become pregnant with Bethy."

"I'm so sorry, Roberta!" Vicky's voice was filled with the pain of her own experience of miscarriage and the death of a child.

"Are you here to speak about Bethy?" Roberta wiped the tears that had sprung into her eyes on her shirt. Being cuffed to the table restricted her from using her hands to wipe her face.

"Would that be okay?" Vicky asked her.

"Yes," Roberta nodded. "I think I'd like that."

"Roberta, you said it took you three attempts to get pregnant with Bethany?" Vicky frowned.

"Yes," Roberta nodded. "The first two times my babies were stillborn."

Vicky looked at Roberta, trying not to show any other emotion other than empathy for a mother that had gone through hell fighting for her daughter's life only to lose her. Vicky hadn't been lying about her attempts at having a child. Nor had she lied about Angel. It had been only the third time Vicky had ever spoken about her attempts to become a parent. Roberta was responding to Vicky as a mother who'd lost a child, and Vicky didn't want to break that connection.

"You actually carried the babies to term, and they were still-born?" Vicky's eyes filled with sorrow. "That's awful."

"I didn't want to believe the doctors at first. You know, each time I had a scan just a day before I gave birth, and the baby was fine. Even healthy." Roberta frowned, and her eyes were shadowed. "I don't understand what happened. But the doctor who delivered my babies told me the first time the umbilical cord had somehow wrapped around the baby's neck. The second time she said the baby's heart had just stopped." She swallowed, and her eyes misted once again. "Then Bethany was born with a heart defect."

"Gosh, Roberta, that is such a lot to have had to go through on your own," Vicky sympathized.

"I wasn't on my own," Roberta told her.

Vicky frowned. "Roberta, do you mind if I ask where you went for your prenatal care?"

"No," Roberta shook her head. "I don't mind you asking. I tried to sue them, you know?" She shook her head. "After my second baby was stillborn. But they sent their sleazy lawyer after me and told me that if I retracted my case, they would make sure the third time would take." Her eyes narrowed angrily. "But I had to also hand over all the documentation I had taken from their offices."

"Roberta, before I get back to the documentation," Vicky leaned forward. "Can you confirm for me that you actually paid for IUI treatment at a fertility clinic?"

"I did," Roberta confirmed. "I can also prove it. Did you know they said I broke into their clinic and stole the samples that they used to help me have my babies?"

"I do know," Vicky nodded. "I want to go over that with you as well if that's okay with you and you don't mind talking about it."

"I don't mind," Roberta told Vicky. "They think I signed their stupid NDA, but I'm not as gullible nor desperate as those other poor women that terrible place was misleading."

"No, you are not," Vicky agreed with Roberta. "Roberta, can you write the name of the clinic on this notepad for me?"

Vicky held the notepad and pen for the guards standing in the room to see. The one came over and inspected it before giving Vicky permission to hand it to Roberta. Roberta used it to write the information Vicky wanted. Roberta turned the paper upside down and pushed it back towards Vicky with the pen.

Vick read the information. The name of the clinic was

written on the paper, along with a familiar address and a six-digit number.

"What is this?" Vicky asked Roberta, looking up at her in shock.

Roberta wouldn't say anything; she just looked from left to right to where the guards were standing. Vicky gave a small nod in understanding.

"It's the address of the clinic?" Vicky covered up because Roberta didn't seem to trust the guards.

Roberta nodded and gave Vicky a grateful smile.

"Roberta, can you tell me about your third pregnancy?" Vicky turned the page on the notepad as if she was going to jot down notes on a new page.

She glanced at Justin, who had not said a word yet. He'd recognized the rapport Vicky had set with Roberta and let her run with it. Justin knew what Vicky wanted him to do.

"Roberta, do you mind if Justin, who you can trust because I do, goes to the clinic to check it out while we talk?" Vicky asked her.

Once again, Roberta looked surprised that someone in Vicky's position was asking her instead of just going ahead and prying through her life.

"No," Roberta shook her head. "I don't mind." Her eyes went to Justin. "You can't trust your cousin, though."

"Ty?" Justin asked Roberta.

"No, the other one." Roberta looked at Vicky. "You shouldn't trust her either, Vicky. She works for the enemy alongside that sleazy lawyer and his niece."

Justin's eyes widened. Vicky saw a flicker of anger in Justin's eyes, and she shook her head in warning. She watched him physically bring his temper under control, and he turned to Roberta.

"Why do you say that, Roberta?" Justin asked her. "Please, if you could elaborate for me because I need to know if someone is trying to sabotage our investigation."

"If I tell you, will you promise you'll help all those other women?" Roberta shocked Justin by saying. "I tried to." She swallowed. "But my Bethy paid the price for it." Her voice dropped. "And Dustin too."

"What?" Vicky and Justin said at the same time, staring wide-eyed at Roberta.

But Roberta clammed up and looked from one guard in the room to the other.

"The walls have eyes and ears!" Roberta told them. "It's better that you go to the clinic. I'm sure they have all the information you need." She looked pointedly at Justin.

"Can you get the guards out of here?" Vicky asked him. "I'm sure I'm safe with Roberta." She looked at Roberta. "Is that correct, Roberta?"

Roberta shook her head and held up her hands as far as she could. "I'm shackled."

Justin agreed to it. He picked up his phone from the table, saying, "Be sure to share the rest of your recording with me, please." He knocked Vicky's pen off the desk and bent to pick it up. "I'll have to take this and the book." Justin told her as he stood and whispered, "1-2-3-4-5."

"Original," Vicky whispered back and shook her head.

"I'm an original kinda guy," Justin grinned and pocketed the phone he'd taken from the desk as well as Vicky's notepad. "I'll let you know what I find at the clinic." He stopped and looked at Vicky. "Do you mind if I ask Lee to help us get a warrant?"

"I'm sure Judge Harkem will be happy to help you," Roberta told Justin. "He'll do whatever it takes to wash his guilt away."

"Good to know," Justin frowned.

"Use whoever you can get the warrant," Vicky told him.

Justin left the room, taking the guards with him.

Vicky ran her fingers over the small device she had in her pocket that was jamming the signals into or out of the room.

"We're secure now, Roberta," Vicky assured her.

Vicky punched the code Justin had given her in the phone on the desk. The recording app was still open but paused. Vicky hit record to start the recording again.

"Can we get back to your third pregnancy?" Vicky asked Roberta.

"It was the roughest one yet," Roberta told Vicky. "I was so sick I was going into the clinic nearly every second day."

"Did the doctors tell you why?" Vicky asked her.

"No, all they seemed to care about was that the baby was healthy," Roberta told her. "Then a work colleague of mine told me that I should let one of the doctors at the hospital check me out."

"You worked at Lower Keys Medical Center, right?" Vicky looked at Roberta.

"Yes." Vicky nodded. "The OBGYN there was appalled that the doctors at the clinic hadn't picked up on the chord or the heart problem of my previous pregnancies."

"Bethany was born at the hospital where you worked?" Vicky clarified.

"She was," Roberta smiled. "Dr. Shier saved Bethy and me. She immediately took me on as a patient even though she was fully booked." Her eyes darkened. "She was a good person. An angel. But that evil lawyer and his team took care of her as well."

"Did Dr. Shier know why you were so sick?" Vicky frowned.

"She said it was the prenatal vitamins that were causing it," Roberta told Vicky. "I came off them right away. Dr. Shier was also convinced that they may have caused Bethy's heart defect."

"What did the clinic say about you switching doctors?" Vicky asked her.

"There wasn't much they could say," Roberta told Vicky. "Not this time around, anyway. They were shocked to find out that I didn't sign their stupid NDA, nor did I sign another one of the crazy contracts they wanted me to sign." She gave a small laugh. "They were so busy trying to make me drop my lawsuit that they didn't realize the forms I filled in were all nonsense."

"How long were you a paying customer of the clinic?" Vicky looked at Roberta.

"About four years," Roberta shocked Vicky by saying. "I used up all the inheritance I got from my father to pay for their crazy research and treatments just to have my baby girl." Her eyes misted over, and she sniffed. "Just to have them take her away from me to a place where I have to wait until my day comes to be with her again."

"Roberta, what these people did to you..." Vicky swallowed; her heart went out to Roberta.

She knew Roberta was a serial arsonist, but the woman had also had nothing but abuse her entire life, it seemed. From an alcoholic mother that had drunk herself to an early grave and a father that punished her in the most horrific ways like locking her in a closet for a day and branding her with a hot fire poker. The man had been a monster.

"Do you still have a copy of those contracts?" Vicky asked her.

"You're not allowed to take the contract from the clinic away with you," Roberta explained. "It violates their confidentiality agreement."

"So, you don't have any proof of the first two contracts you signed?" Vicky looked at Roberta questioningly.

"I didn't say that," Roberta corrected Vicky. "I don't think any of those other poor trusting mothers did, though." Her eyes blazed. "You know, we went to that clinic because of the reputation. It was supposed to be one of the top fertility clinics." She shook her head. "Well, when they tried to steal Bethy from me, I knew what they'd done or were doing."

"Wait!" Vicky stopped Roberta. "What do you mean they tried to steal Bethy from you?"

"It was my second night in hospital after I had given birth to my Bethy," Roberta explained. "Dr. Shier had told the nurses to let Bethy stay in my room. She was worried about something, but she wouldn't tell me what. I was drifting off to sleep with Bethy sleeping in her crib next to me when someone slipped into my room and tried to take Bethy."

"What did you do?" Vicky asked; the alarm bells were echoing through her head.

"I hit the person over the head with my glass water jug and

rang for attention when I saw a woman in a nurse's uniform crumple to the floor," Roberta told her story. "I recognized her immediately. She was the sales lady from that clinic."

"Sales lady?" Vicky looked at Roberta, confused.

"Oh, yes," Roberta nodded. "She was one of Dustin's mother's friends and is why Dustin's mother told me to go to that clinic."

"Dustin's mother told you to go to the clinic?" Vicky nearly choked on her shock at Roberta's statement. Something Roberta had said earlier sprung to mind. "Roberta, you said you weren't alone through your pregnancies?"

"No, I wasn't," Roberta shook her head. "Aunt Lillian and Aunt Ainsley were helping me."

"Sorry?" Vicky's eyes widened in shock. "They were helping you?"

"Oh, yes," Roberta nodded. "Aunt Ainsley and Aunt Lillian told me to come to Key West and they would help me. I was on the run because I was being accused of my father's murder." She shook her head and looked at Vicky. "Can I tell you a secret?"

"Sure," Vicky nodded.

"They told me they would help Bethy," Roberta's eyes misted over once again. "But they lied. Just like they lied about helping me with Dustin." Tears dropped down Roberta's cheeks. "I'd do anything for Dustin and Bethy, you know?" She looked into Vicky's eyes.

That's when Vicky knew there was a whole lot more to not only the clinic story but the arson story as well. Roberta was covering for someone or a group of people, and Vicky was starting to get a sick feeling in her stomach that she might know who they were.

"Roberta, you know if there are still people out there responsible for Dustin and Bethany's death, you need to tell me so I can help you bring them to justice," Vicky told her. "It's unfair that you have had to suffer all this and take the fall for it on your own when you've already been through so much."

"I tried to bring them to justice, Vicky," Roberta said. "I didn't want to hurt Christy or her family. But I had no choice."

"What do you mean by that?" Vicky asked her.

"I never went to the retirement village to find Christy's grandfather," Roberta admitted to Vicky.

"Why did you go there?" Vicky asked her.

"To find Tarryn Young and Judge Harkem!" Roberta's eyes blazed as she said their names.

"Why those two people?" Vicky asked.

"Tarryn Young was Judge Harkem's secret weapon," Roberta said bitterly. "She was the one the clinic would send around to make sure the families who used the clinic toed the line."

"Are you sure it's Tarryn Young?" Vicky's heartbeat in her throat. "Why would she do that?"

"Maybe you should ask her about Holden, her son!" Roberta raised her eyebrows.

"Are you suggesting that Tarryn was a patient of the clinic?" Alarm bells started ringing in Vicky's head as pieces of another unsolved puzzle started to fall in place.

"I'm not *suggesting* anything," Roberta told Vicky. "I'm telling you what I know and what I can prove."

"Can we go back to the beginning, Roberta?" Vicky looked at her watch. "I need to know everything."

Roberta looked up at Vicky and nodded, "Will you promise to bury me next to my Bethy?"

"Are you sick?" Vicky looked at Roberta in alarm.

"No," Roberta shook her head. "But if I tell you everything, I'll become a target, just like my friend Samantha Harvey was."

"You knew Samantha Harvey?" Vicky breathed.

"Yes, she and Christy's lost sister-in-law were helping me," Roberta frowned. "Although I don't think she was who she claimed to be. But she did look a lot like her."

"Christy's sister-in-law?" Vicky's brows drew together in confusion before realization dawned on her. "Are you talking about...?"

"I hear she turned herself in," Roberta informed Vicky. "Two days after I was arrested."

"That's who was in my father's office!" Vicky shook her head. "Roberta, you said you had no choice but to go after Christy's family. Can you explain that to me?"

"I had to get Tarryn to back off," Roberta told her. "Those people had to pay. For everyone they hurt. They were a stain on this earth."

"Roberta, why didn't you come forward with this instead of taking justice into your own hands?" Vicky asked her.

"Justice?" Roberta looked at Vicky in disgust. "There is no justice for people like me—the girl from the wrong side of the tracks who was accused of being a monster." She swallowed. "All I wanted to do was to have that perfect life I saw other families have when I was growing up."

"Roberta, you hurt a lot of people and destroyed a lot of property," Vicky said softly. "Not just here in Key West either," she pointed out as delicately as she could. "You hurt Ainsley and Lillian's parents. Ainsley said you were the reason Lillian took her kids and ran."

"And you believed her over me?" Roberta pointed out. "It's always been that way. The only one who stuck up for me or tried to protect me from all those monsters was Dustin."

"Roberta, can you tell me your side of the story?" Vicky had a feeling that Ainsley Krull and Lillian Wright had a lot more to answer for than Ainsley Krull was letting on.

"They were like three sisters, you know," Roberta started to tell her side of the story.

"Three sisters?" Vicky frowned.

"Yes, Aunt Ainsley, Aunt Lillian, and my mother's younger sister, Belinda." Roberta looked at Vicky expectantly.

"What happened to Belinda?" Vicky asked. "I know that Ainsley made her way to Key West, and that is why Lillian eventually moved here."

"Belinda had already made her move to Key West a little

while before Ainsley did," Roberta's eyes held Vicky's gaze. Something in them set off little alarm bells in Vicky's head.

"Is she still here?" Vicky asked, ignoring the horrible feeling that she already knew the answer to that question.

"She got married, had a kid, got divorced, got remarried, and then died," Roberta leaned back in her chair, looking at Vicky with a look on her face that intensified the sick feeling.

"Roberta, what are you trying to tell me?" Vicky tried to keep the annoyance from her voice.

"Did you know we were cousins?" Roberta tilted her head to one side. "Why do you think I would only talk to you?"

"I don't understand?" Vicky said, trying to squash down the nausea and panic rising inside her while storing the bombshell Roberta had just dropped on her for processing when she was done interviewing Roberta. "I requested to talk to you."

"No," Roberta shook her head. "I've been telling your father and Lee Young I'd only speak to you since I was arrested."

Vicky felt the blood drain from her head. She had to steady her breathing and hold on to her emotions that were threatening to overwhelm her. More pieces of this weird twisted case started to fall into place. The return of Tilly, Tarryn, and Robin pushing Vicky to let her come with her to Key West. Another horrible thought struck her, and her heart stopped in her chest when she realized everyone she'd thought she could trust, she couldn't. Not even....

"Justin!" Vicky's eyes grew wide. "Did I just send him into the arms of the enemy?" She looked up at Roberta.

"Don't worry, he won't go to who you think he will," Roberta told Vicky. "Justin knows who the two of you can trust."

"Again, what do you mean?" Vicky was getting really tired of games and being kept in the dark.

"Justin and I have had a few private talks," Roberta admitted to Vicky. "Why do you think I spoke to you in front of him?"

"You said that if you talked, your life wouldn't be safe," Vicky looked worriedly at Roberta.

"Justin has been making sure I'm safe for now," Roberta told

Vicky. "Don't worry about me, Vicky." She leaned forward. "I wasn't going to hurt Christy or her family," she said softly. "But I had to show a certain person that I was serious about bringing the truth forward and cleansing the earth from those foul beings."

"Roberta," Vicky swallowed nervously. "Are you talking about Tarryn Young?" she said wide-eyed. "Or are there more Youngs involved?"

"It all starts and ends with the Youngs," Roberta said softly. "Ask Jack; he found that out the hard way."

"You need to start at the beginning, Roberta," Vicky's hands shook as she dropped them into her lap to get control of herself. "I need to know everything."

"I'm glad you managed to get here today for this," Roberta smiled sadly at Vicky. "Because tomorrow I'm being taken to that maximum-security prison where Samantha died. I needed to tell you what I've been trying to tell you for a while now."

Vicky's eyes widened in shock as she stared at Roberta. "It was you?" she said softly. "You're the one that was sending me those anonymous notes?"

"You needed help and not the kind you were getting from those you thought you could trust," Roberta told her.

"Thank you," Vicky gave Roberta a small smile. "But, now I need you to tell me your whole story." She glanced at the door. "But first, there's something I have to do."

"No," Roberta raised her voice. "Vicky, don't!"

"I need to get you out of here," Vicky told her. "Your life is in danger, and quite frankly, if we are going to solve and get to the bottom of all this, we need you alive." She looked at Roberta. "Don't you want to get justice for those parents the clinic wronged and for Dustin and Bethany?"

"I will," Roberta assured Vicky. "Because I know you will do it for me." She gave Vicky a sad smile. "My life wasn't always bad." She told Vicky. "I had a baby brother, you know."

"You did?" Vicky sat down against her better judgment.

"Yes," Roberta nodded. "You know how I knew without a shadow of a doubt that I could trust you?"

"No," Vicky shook her head.

"Because you saved his life," Roberta shocked Vicky by saying. "My mother wasn't always a drunk, and my father wasn't always a monster."

Vicky said nothing. She sat and listened to Roberta tell her life story. By the time she was done, a lump was burning a hole in Vicky's throat as she'd swallowed it down. She was a hardened agent. Vicky had seen and done things that would make most people's toes curl. But Roberta's story tore Vicky's heart and almost reduced her to a puddle of salty tears on the floor.

"Thank you, Roberta," Vicky cleared her throat, leaned forward, and covered Roberta's hands with her own. "I'm sorry we never got to know each other. You've filled so many holes in my case. But you opened the door for me and gave me insight into a cold case." She swallowed. "I'm going to make sure you are protected."

"Vicky," Roberta gave her hand a gentle squeeze. "I've accepted my fate, my punishment, and made peace with my sins." She smiled. "All I ask is that you lay me to rest next to my Bethy and near my hero."

"No," Vicky shook her head. "I'm not letting you die without seeing how all you've told me here today is going to help those who've been wronged and get justice for your daughter and Dustin."

"I've already done all I can," Roberta assured Vicky. "Thank you, Vicky, for giving my baby brother and me a chance when everyone else just turned their backs on us." She let go of Vicky's hand. "Please tell Justin that I said thank you for believing in me too. I hope he finds the answer he's looking for. The witness Justin's partner has will answer a lot of Lee Young's questions too."

"I can still get you out of here, Roberta," Vicky told her. "Just say the word."

"No," Roberta shook her head. "I need you to be able to move freely and not have to hide because you saved me."

"Look, I'm going to talk to Justin," Vicky promised her.

"Okay," Roberta sighed and shook her head. "You need to go now. You have a lot of work to do."

"I'll come to see you again," Vicky assured Roberta.

"You might want to start by making up with Lee Young," Roberta grinned. "You're going to need him."

"I know!" Vicky sighed before calling the guards.

As they took Roberta away, Vicky stopped them. "If one hair gets harmed on her head, you'd better learn to sleep with one eye open," she warned them.

The guard's eyes grew wide, but both of them nodded before marching Roberta back to her cell.

Vicky stood staring down the hallway for a few minutes, her mind reeling with all the information Roberta had given her. She had a lot of work to do, but Roberta was right, and Vicky needed Lee's help. She could take the cowardly way out and ask Justin to help her with that, but she knew it was time to face the music and get Lee to dance with her again.

A smile split her lips as an idea came to her. She picked up her phone to make a call and realized she didn't have her phone. Justin had swapped it to get Garry's number and make sure he'd answer Justin's call. Vicky was about to call Justin when a calendar reminder popped up on his phone.

Emily's Day!

Vicky frowned. Was the reminder referring to Emily Jones? Emily had been Justin's first big love. Vicky and Christy had actually thought that Justin would settle down with Emily; he was so smitten with her. But after several years of dating, Emily just vanished from Justin's life. When Justin was asked about her, he'd simply say that things didn't work out between them.

Vicky bit her lip as she wondered what happened to Emily and why Justin had a calendar event that repeated on the same day every year called Emily's Day. Before Vicky could think further on the subject, Justin called her.

"Hello," Vicky answered his phone. "I have a lot to tell you, but we're going to need Lee's help."

"I know," Justin said from the other end of the phone. "I found all the information Roberta has. You need to come and take a look at this."

"I'm on my way; I just need to make a stop at Lee's office first," Vicky told him.

"No, he's on his way too," Justin assured her. "I took the liberty of messaging him on your behalf."

"Excuse me?" Vicky hissed into the phone. "You did what?"

"He's on his way and will be here in ten minutes, so you need to get here in five," Justin told her, then hung up so she couldn't argue with him.

Vicky clenched her jaw and stalked out of the building towards her car, thinking of all the way she was going to kill Justin Young.

SHADOWS OF YESTERDAY DARKEN TODAY

Lee wasn't expecting to see Justin's car at the address Vicky had sent him to meet her at. Lee had been pleasantly surprised to get a message from Vicky. He'd wanted to call her for three days now but had been so busy at work, and he'd hardly gotten time to breathe. The DA's office had charged Lee with finding his replacement, and between that and the caseload he had to try to divide between the other attorneys to finalize, he'd been working around the clock.

Lee was tired and frustrated at not having enough hours in the day to look into the information he'd been gathering from the conversation he and Vicky had with Judge Harkem. Lee was also desperate to talk to Vicky and apologize for accusing her without giving her a chance to explain. But mostly, he was longing to see her, hear her voice, feel her warm smile brighten his day, and have an ear to listen to his concerns about Jessie and Oliver.

Lee hadn't given one thought to the pile of work on his desk when Vicky had asked him to meet in ten minutes. He'd just pushed it aside and rushed out the door. His mind was filled with things to say to her. As soon as he'd seen Justin's car at the same address, all those words he'd rehearsed on the way over had blown away like an untied helium balloon. Lee had been so distracted with getting to see Vicky he hadn't even realized the significance of the address Vicky wanted to meet him at.

As Lee climbed out of his car, he looked up at the neat house. It was a house that had once belonged to Christy and Dustin. He glanced at the real estate sign on the lawn. Lee's heart lurched when he saw that the For Sale sign sported a big red Sold across it. Surely Vicky hadn't bought Christy's old house? Why on earth would she invite Lee and Justin to see it? Lee walked up the front stairs of the house and was about to knock when the door creaked open.

"Hello?" Lee called, stepping inside. "Vicky?" Lee walked through the front hallway and looked into the living room. It was empty. "Justin?" he called, but there was no answer.

Lee glanced up the stairs, standing quietly to hear if he could hear movement. There was none. His frown deepened as he walked into the kitchen. The back door was standing wide open. Lee looked outside and saw a shed.

"Well, that's new," Lee said, noticing the door to the shed was slightly ajar.

Lee walked towards the shed and stopped when he heard voices coming from inside.

"You don't have to do this," Lee's heart did a flip when he heard Vicky's voice.

Lee quietly drew nearer as his danger senses started to tingle.

"Look, I just want the both of you to turn around and leave," a very familiar female voice said.

Lee froze. *What on earth was going on?* He peered into the window, and his heart stopped in his chest at the scene he saw. Before he could be noticed, he jumped back out of view.

This can't be happening! Lee thought to himself. *Has everyone gone crazy?*

"We can't do that," Lee heard Justin say. "If you just drop the gun, we can talk this through. You know that there's nothing we can't solve together."

"Not this time, Justin," the familiar female voice said. Lee's blood ran cold from the tone of her voice. It was flat and deadly.

In all the years he'd known her, he'd never heard her sound so... unemotional!

Lee knew he had to do something and fast. Whatever it was that Vicky and Justin wouldn't give up, Lee had no doubt that the woman holding that gun wouldn't hesitate to shoot them.

"There's a lot more going on here and at stake than any of you know," the woman said to Justin and Vicky. "Now, please, turn around and walk away."

"That's not going to happen," Justin warned. "You know you're outnumbered, right?"

"Yes, but I'm the one holding the loaded gun, and the rest of Vicky's band of merry misfits are off on a wild goose chase," the woman pointed out to them. "And your people, Justin, aren't on the side you think they are."

Lee knew he had to act fast, and there was only one option. He'd seen how close the woman holding the gun was standing to the door. Lee knew there was a risk to what he was about to do. He just hoped his brother and Vicky's reflexes were as good as agents of their stature were trained to be.

Before Lee could give it a second thought, he rammed the door as hard as he could, sending it into the back of the woman with the gun. Lee heard Justin shout, "Vicky, watch out." There was a gunshot, and Lee skidded to a stop in time to see Justin tackle Vicky to the floor.

A roaring in his ears nearly deafened him when Lee saw Justin roll-off Vicky and lie on his back. Blood soaked Justin's shirt near his shoulder. Lee's eyes pivoted towards Vicky, who was lying so still on the floor. Her shirt was also soaked in blood. Lee was about to drop to his knees on the floor when Vicky's eyes flew open and met Lee's.

"Go after her!" Vicky said breathlessly. "Quickly, before she gets away."

"But you're hurt!" Lee said, feeling like his heart had stopped beating when he saw all the blood on Vicky's shirt.

"No, I'm not!" Vicky grumbled. "I think Justin cracked my rib when he landed on me."

"But the blood..." Lee said, dumbfounded, and his eyes traveled to Justin, who was lying on the floor. "Justin's been shot!" he breathed.

Vicky shot up, wincing as she pushed herself forward. "Justin!" Her voice sounded frantic. "You big oaf!" She looked at him. "Speak to me."

"Go..." Justin looked at Vicky, "after her." he managed to get out. "Now..."

"Don't talk," Vicky pulled off her sweater and put pressure on Justin's wound with it before pulling out her phone with her free hand. She looked up at Lee. "Go after her!" Vicky ordered.

Lee nodded, turned, and dashed out of the shed when he heard the sound of a motorbike starting up in the lane. He turned and ran towards it.

"Tarryn!" Lee shouted. "Stop!"

Tarryn Young turned towards Lee and flipped the visor of her helmet up, "Look after Holden for me, and keep him away from his father."

"Tarryn, don't do this," Lee started to walk towards the dirt bike she was on. "Please."

"I need you to promise me you will look after Holden and keep him away from his father!" Tarryn's eyes were cold as she stared at Lee.

"I promise," Lee promised.

Tarryn nodded, flipped her visor down, and took off. Lee stood gaping after her, wondering when his life had gotten so turned upside down. The sound of sirens screaming towards the house caught his attention, and he ran towards them.

Lee pointed the paramedics towards the shed and waited for Ty, who was running towards him.

"What happened?" Ty asked Lee.

"You're not going to believe me," Lee put his arm on Ty's shoulders and walked him through to the shed. "But your sister shot Justin."

"You're joking, right?" Ty's brows furrowed as he stared at Lee in disbelief.

Lee swallowed and shook his head, "I wish I was."

Lee walked with Ty into the shed where the medics were working on Justin, and Vicky was refusing treatment as she barked out orders to them.

"Vicky," Ty ran up to her. "What is going on?"

"Let's see," Vicky glared at Ty. "Your sister just tried to kill us, and she stole some vital evidence before running away." Her eyes narrowed into angry slits. "Please tell me you don't have anything to do with whatever your sister is involved in."

"Vicky, I swear to you I don't," Ty assured her. "I thought that...." He swallowed.

"I told you a long time ago I had concerns about her," Vicky's anger turned to fury. She bent down to pick up her stained sweater, wincing at the pain in her ribs.

"You're hurt!" Ty dashed forward to help her, but she pushed him away.

"Don't!" She held up her hand. "I'll deal with you later. I don't want your forensics' team here. Is that clear?" she hissed at Ty.

"You know I have to report this?" Ty pointed out.

"I already have, and it is now officially an FBI case," Vicky glanced around the room. "As is everything that is in this shed is now my evidence."

"What is this?" Ty looked around the room.

"I'm not sure if I can trust you with that right now," Vicky said to him. "Lee," she turned to look at him. "Can you ride with Justin to the hospital?"

"I'll go," Ty volunteered. "It looks like you're going to need some help here."

"My team is on their way," Vicky assured Ty.

"No, Lee..." Ty turned towards his cousin. "I'll go with Justin. You stay and help Vicky." He turned back to Vicky. "If my sister did this, I'll find her." He promised Vicky and Lee. "She's had her free pass."

Ty turned towards Lee. "I'm sorry, brother!" he said to Lee before walking past Lee and following the paramedics pushing Justin towards the ambulance.

"What did he mean by all that?" Lee walked over to Vicky, who looked at the drawer of the filing cabinet that Tarryn had yanked a few files out of.

"It's a long story," Vicky told Lee. She had her hands over her ribs as she pushed the drawer closed. "I need to secure this shed and get all this stuff moved to a safer location immediately."

"Can I help?" Lee asked her.

"I'd like that," Vicky looked up at him and smiled.

Lee knew at that moment Vicky was holding up her own olive branch. "I would too." He smiled back down at her.

Lee and Vicky worked together over the next hour loading Vicky's SUV with all the information that was in the shed. As they worked, Vicky explained to Lee that the shed and Christy's old house now belonged to Roberta Davies.

Vicky went on to tell Lee that the FBI had asked her to look into Samantha Harvey, who they told her was wanted for killing her fiancé after her two former husbands had died under mysterious circumstances. Vicky had found out that Samantha was working for the DA's office where Lee was working. There were a lot of red flags on the file Vicky had been given and more so when the FBI database seemed to have limited information on the case.

Vicky had taken the case when she'd found out where Samantha worked and who Samantha was dating. Vicky had become even more alarmed when one of her agents told her that they had reason to believe that Samantha Harvey wasn't who she was claiming to be. Vicky had reason to believe that Samantha was, in fact, a woman named Cordelia Watson, a ruthless and deadly black widow agent. The black widows were a team of elite erasers that cleaned up the mess of anyone or any corporation. They weren't fussy about who their clients were. But they were serious about completing their missions.

The minute Vicky was told who Samantha really was, she'd become even more suspicious about the case she'd been given or the reasons she'd been given the case. Vicky had been even more alarmed when Jessie had shown up to their lunch meeting with a highly classified file of Samantha's. Vicky had eventually managed to get Jessie to admit a day ago that she and Oliver had seen Tarryn give the file to Robin Kelly, one of Vicky's team. Tarryn had given it to Robin the day before Vicky was given the case file for her case. Only the folder that Tarryn had was the real file on Samantha Harvey. The file Vicky had in her possession had been tampered with by Robin and Tarryn.

Vicky admitted to having a plan for breaking Samantha and Lee's relationship up. But it hadn't been the one Jessie had set in motion. Vicky wanted Jessie and her to try talking him out of it. Vicky had advised Jessie that they needed to let Lee see the file Jessie had given Vicky. They were going to do it that night at the restaurant. Jessie was going to ask Lee and Samantha if they would join the three of them at dinner. Then Jessie was going to ask Lee if she could have a word in private with him. Vicky would follow and show Lee the file. But Jessie had completely disregarded Vicky's plan and raged ahead with hers.

"I'm so sorry about what happened that night, Lee," Vicky looked up at him. "I should've told you at dinner or called you the next day."

"It's okay," Lee assured her with a warm smile. "I owe you an apology too," he admitted. "I was so scared of what I felt for you, I jumped at the first excuse to push you away." He took a step closer to her.

"Oh?" Vicky looked up at him and took a step towards him.

"I'm sorry, I didn't give you a chance to explain and judged you on the spot," Lee stepped closer and was right in front of her. "I was an idiot. But in my defense, love makes fools of even the greatest person."

"Okay...." Vicky smiled up at him. "Go on."

"You're not going to make this easy for me, are you?" Lee cupped her face in his hands.

"No," Vicky shook her head. "But I might be more lenient if I heard more."

"You've always had your own special place in my heart, Vicky Donovan," Lee said softly. "You've driven me crazy your entire life. I'm so madly in love with you that it scares me to death but at the same time makes me feel like I can move mountains." He lowered his face towards hers. "And I know as long as I have you in my life, it will be complete."

His lips touched hers, and their hearts beat in tune as Vicky wound her arms around his neck. She pulled away and rested her forehead against his, "I love you too, Lee Young." Her eyes sparkled with love for him. "Why do you think I was such an annoyance to you when I was young? I had such a giant crush on you. I made every excuse I could to be around you." She gave a soft laugh. "Then I came back to Key West and saw you might be a target for a deadly assassin. I knew I'd do whatever it took to keep you safe. I love you so much that I couldn't picture another moment without you in my life."

Lee pulled her to him as their lips joined once again. They were standing in Vicky's father's office, which was soon to be his office. Lee and Vicky had moved all the evidence from Roberta's shed into the safest place they knew. Shaun Donovan's office vault. The world around them faded away, making them forget that there were people waiting for them in the boardroom.

"Excuse me," a soft female voice that he knew all too well and hadn't heard in years brought reality crashing back on Lee and Vicky. "I know this is a bad time. But if you don't come now, I'm going to kill that neanderthal that you left me with, Vicky!"

Lee and Vicky drew apart, and Lee turned towards the office door.

"Matty?" Lee stared at his baby sister in shock. "Matty!" he said again and rushed forward, scooping his tiny sister up into his arms. "When did you get back to Key West?"

"Uh..." Matty wiggled in his arms. "Lee..." she breathed. "You're crushing me."

"Oh," Lee put Matty down. "I always forget how tiny you are."

"Thanks!" Matty grinned at her brother. "But I'm going to let your reference to my size slide because it's so good to see you." She wrapped her arms around Lee's waist for a hug. She stepped back and looked up at Lee. "How's Hannah? I couldn't believe how grown up she is."

"Matty..." Lee began but was cut off when Special Agent Garry, who Lee now knew not only worked with Vicky but was her cousin, walked into the office.

"Don't you have ears, Tiny Tilly?" Special Agent Garry growled at Matty.

Lee's big brother instincts kicked in. He didn't care who the man was. No one talked to his sisters like that. "Watch your tone around my sister," he warned.

"Well then, maybe you should babysit her and keep her out of the clutches of the people who are after her," Garry looked at Lee, completely unfazed by Lee's threat.

"What people are after you, Matty?" Lee looked down at Matty with worry shining in his eyes.

"Oh, it's nothing," Matty brushed it off. "I want to hear about Hannah."

"Can we keep the family reunion for another time?" Garry suggested. "Right now, there's a witness that we need information from." He glared at Matty. "Information that can help you so I can be free of you!"

"Free of me?" Matty's eyes blazed as she spun out of Lee's arms and advanced on the man who stood towering over her. "Do you think I want to live in a smelly swamp with the swamp creature?"

"Okay!" Vicky stepped in between them. "Enough." She looked at the two of them. "We need to get into the boardroom, and I haven't had a chance to prep Lee yet."

Garry and Matty stopped glaring at each other to turn and looked at Lee wide-eyed.

"Okay." Matty started to step back towards the door, bumping into Garry.

They looked at each other, back at Lee, and then both bolted out the door. Matty stopped, stuck her head back in to say to Lee, "I love you big brother... oh, and I'm going by Tilly now." Then she ducked back out of the door.

"What was all that about?" Lee stood staring at Vicky.

"Unbelievable," Vicky was looking at the empty doorway. "Those two cowards just threw me under the bus." She looked up at Lee.

"You know, I'm not even going to ask," Lee sighed. "These past weeks, everything has just gotten weirder and weirder in my world."

"Well, it's going to get a lot more so," Vicky told him quietly. "Lee, I can explain about Matty... sorry, Tilly."

"Vicky," Lee walked forward and pulled her to him. "It's about time you let people answer for themselves. I want to hear it from her. It shouldn't have to come from you. You carry too many people's troubles on your shoulders. Trying to help or save them." He kissed her on the forehead. "Who saves you?" he said softly.

"You!" Vicky smiled up at him. "You saved me from trapping my heart away when I thought my world had died with Grant."

"You save me too, Vicky," Lee said softly. "You pulled me out of the frozen tundra of numbness and back into the warmth of your love."

"You have such a way with words, counselor," Vicky told him teasingly. She kissed him gently on the lips before pulling away. "But, Lee, there's something that may just make you feel differently."

"I don't think anything could," Lee admitted.

"Lee," Vicky took a deep breath before stepping out of his arms. "We have a witness in the boardroom that we need some answers from. We believe that the person has information about the clinics and KW Research facility that can help up with this case Roberta has now brought to our attention."

"Okay!" Lee's eyes narrowed as he watched Vicky. She seemed nervous.

"We believe that the clinic has been stealing children," Vicky shocked him by saying. "And this has been going on for decades."

"What?" Lee felt his heart drop to his feet and a sick feeling rose in his stomach.

As a parent, whenever he came across a case of a missing child, he'd feel physically ill for the parents. Knowing how it felt to have his wife disappear, Lee never wanted to imagine what it would feel like to have his baby girl stolen away from him.

"They started out stealing kids around the age of two," Vicky explained. "Like your father's older sister." She reminded him of the conversation with Judge Harkem. "They targeted families that had twins or kids that were eleven to fifteen months apart."

"That's horrible," Lee breathed.

"Yes, but that drew too much attention, especially after one kidnapping was traced back to KW Research Labs," Vicky explained. "Whoever these people are, they turned to a new venture. They opened fertility and parent's wellness hospitals."

"The clinics Roberta told you about," Lee guessed.

"Yes," Vicky confirmed. "Only they are no longer stealing two-year-olds. They are stealing newborn babies."

"Babies?" Lee choked.

"Yes, the parents of the clinic are given all this extra special care and attention at the clinic," Vicky explained. "They target families that are desperate to have kids or more kids." Her eyes narrowed as she continued. "Their prices are so good, and they offer all this outstanding care at good prices because they are funding most of it by selling babies to families that have no chance of ever conceiving a child."

"I take it that the parents buying the child don't know that they are getting a stolen child?" Lee asked.

"No," Vicky shook her head. "They think they are paying for a surrogate that has been vetted and recommended by the clinic. "The clinic gets a fee for finding the surrogate, and then couples waiting for the baby pay for the surrogate's care at the clinic."

"Meanwhile, the parents actually having the child are paying for the clinic to take care of all their prenatal needs," Lee guessed. A spurt of red-hot anger blazed through his stomach.

"Yes," Vicky said. "But that's not all."

"How much more disgusting can this clinic get?" Lee breathed.

"How about how they get donors for IUI treatments that offer to want to be parents like Roberta?" Vicky said. "Usually, donor clinics pay for the donors. But the clinic found a way to have their donors, both men and women, pay them for their denotations."

"I don't know if I want to hear this," Lee growled. "I'm ready to march down to that clinic and put everyone involved in jail."

"We can't do that either," Vicky said. "We can't use any of Roberta's evidence. She broke into the clinic and stole it. We had agents raid each of the clinics spread throughout Florida, but they were squeaky clean. So, we have a leak somewhere within our circle."

"How do we find out who that is?" Lee asked her.

"By allowing our undercover agents to do what they do best," Vicky grinned. "Get hard evidence."

"But how do you know who to trust to do that?" Lee asked.

"We'll speak about that soon," Vicky assured him. "But right now, we have someone waiting who has spent many years trying to get information about the clinic, and the person will only talk to you."

"Why?" Lee asked.

"Before we go in," Vicky said softly. "I want you to know that I'm madly in love with you, and I know the next few minutes are going to be a huge shock for you. I understand that you will have mixed emotions."

Vicky started walking Lee towards the boardroom.

"Nothing can change how I feel for you, Vicky," Lee tried to assure her.

"I wouldn't be too sure about that," Vicky said, standing at the door of the boardroom. "I'm sorry, Lee," she whispered as she pushed the door open.

Lee frowned down at Vicky, who stepped aside so Lee could step into the room. He had this strange feeling he was stepping into a lion's den. The room was deadly quiet as Lee turned his eyes and scanned the people in the room. Shaun Donovan, Luke, Lee's nephew, Matty, and Garry sat staring at him. His frown deepened in confusion as to why Vicky would've said what she did, and his heart froze in his chest as a soft voice called his name from behind him.

"Hello, Lee!" There was no mistaking that voice. He'd played it over and over again in his head so many times.

Lee swung around. His eyes locked with the big green eyes of a woman who'd been lost to him for twenty-eight years. "Georgia?" Lee managed to get out when he could finally breathe again.

Lee was so shocked to see Georgia standing in front of him that he didn't notice Vicky slip out of the room.

EPILOGUE

"So, after all that," Justin said, sitting in his hospital bed. "She won't help us or give us the information we need until we help her find her daughter?"

"Yup," Vicky nodded. "At least that's what she told Lee."

"How did he take the fact that she has an eleven-year-old daughter?" Justin asked.

"It's been a long time, Justin," Vicky said. "I'm sure even Lee would realize that Georgia wouldn't stay single forever."

"Dawn!" Justin corrected. "Her name is Dawn now."

"Of course," Vicky shook her head. "But my dad was right. It's hard to call her by another name when we know her as Georgia."

"She was in protective custody for a long time until she disappeared from us too," Justin told Vicky. "I still wonder what made her run away from protective custody?" He looked at Vicky.

"That's something to look into for another day," Vicky told him. "What Dawn did tell us, though, was that Samantha Harvey was helping her find her sister that was stolen at birth from the same clinic. Dawn's mother heard her baby cry and was alert enough to see a sister take a wriggly baby from the room before the doctors sedated her."

"So, Dawn had a sister!" Justin looked surprised. "A sister who she believes was taken by the clinic?" He shook his head. "The clinic couldn't have been too pleased to find out that Dawn's mother remembered the incident?" Justin said.

"They were quick to cover it up," Vicky said to Justin. "They told Dawn's mother that it was because of the pain drugs they gave her. She'd had a reaction that had made her hallucinate. But Dawn's mother wouldn't give up the search to find the truth. Dawn believes it's the reason they killed her parents when Dawn was sixteen."

"Is that what Dawn was researching at KW Labs?" Justin asked.

"When Dawn was twenty, the people who were renting her parent's mansion moved out, and she was able to go back into it," Vicky explained. "Dawn found all her mother's journals and research there. Information Judge Harkem was supposed to destroy."

"What is up with Judge Harkem?" Justin frowned. "What is his involvement in all this other than nearly having lost a niece?"

"He was coerced, shall we say, into defending the clinic and KW Research Labs." She raised her eyebrows. "Judge Harkem put Samantha's sister into the DA's office as Samantha Harvey to protect your family and to get the FBI involved in the case."

"Why, if he was defending the clinic and KW Research Labs, would he want the FBI poking around?" Justin asked. "Surely he realized he was implicating himself?"

"I don't think he cares, not when he has stage four cancer," Vicky told Justin. "Also, he couldn't come forward with the information because of attorney-client privileges and all that. So, he needed another way to get the authorities involved in opening a case against the clinic, and I think KW Research labs as well."

"Clever!" Justin said. "He knew that Samantha would be identified as a fraud, and it would lead back to his niece's case, and if it landed in your hands, you'd crack the case wide open."

"I think so," Vicky said. "But my agent and your cousin intercepted it. I think they've been waiting for this to happen. So, they switched out the information in the file only to have my agent's son and your niece overhear Robin and Tarryn. Oliver found the file, copied it, and gave it to the love of his life, Jessie."

"So, you ended up with the real file anyway and a file on who fake Samantha really was," Justin gave a low whistle. "But now both Robin and Tarryn are in the wind, and we don't know who they are working for or what their end game is."

"I do know that the two files Tarryn stole were about her parents and you," Vicky told him.

"What on earth does she want information on me for, and why would Roberta even have information like that?" Justin asked.

"I think you already know the answer to one of those questions, Justin," Vicky said softly. "And please, you need to share it with me because whatever you're going to do, I want you to know that my trusted team and I are right there with you."

"Thank you, Vicky," Justin dropped his act and looked at her. "But I need time to process what's been going on first, and as soon as I have my head sorted out and I'm out of the hospital, we'll continue this conversation."

"Fair enough," Vicky smiled at him. "You have all my resources at your disposal."

"So, your mother was Roberta Davies' sister?" Justin changed the subject.

"Yes," Vicky nodded. "I may not have liked my mother, but at least she'd gotten out of a bad situation as soon as she could. She got a bursary to an excellent law school and married my father."

"Yes, then she threw it all away," Justin reminded her and then stopped. "Sorry!"

"No, you're right!" Vicky said. "Roberta told me that my mother was not too happy to see Ainsley show up in Key West and then some years later Lillian."

"Do you think that maybe your mother didn't leave because she wanted to but because she had to?" Justin asked.

"After speaking to Roberta this morning, the same thought

crossed my mind," Vicky admitted. "Then I found my mother's journals in Roberta's collection."

"Your mother kept journals?" Justin looked at her, surprised. "Your mother always seemed so self-possessed and snobbish. I didn't think she'd do something like that."

"Me either," Vicky agreed with Justin. "But she did. Each entry is meticulously dated and time-stamped."

"Wow," Justin pulled a face. "The only reason someone would usually do that is if they were trying to keep a log of events."

"Like a log of events on Cyril Butler?" Vicky gave Justin a smug smile at the look on his face.

"Wasn't Cyril the one that was arrested on suspicion of taking Judge Harkem's niece?"

"Yes, he was," Vicky nodded. "We also know that both KW Research and the Florida Perfect Parent's Clinic are owned by the same company."

"Let me guess," Justin said. "The Butler Corporation?"

"Yes," Vicky answered.

"Do you think Aaron is involved in all this?" Justin's eyes grew wide.

"I don't want to think so," Vicky looked at Justin. "But we're going to have to look into the possibility."

"I know!" Justin's face fell. "Which begs the obvious question of do we tell Christy?"

"No!" Lee said from the room door, giving Justin and Vicky both a fright.

"How long have you been standing there?" Justin growled, holding his chest. "I'm on a freakin' heart monitor, dude!" He pointed to the device that was showing a spike in his pulse. "Are you trying to scare us to death?"

"Aren't you both some sort of super spies?" Lee looked at them. "I've been standing here for about ten minutes, and neither of you noticed."

"We're not spies!" Justin said impatiently. "Good grief, man."

"Hi, Lee," Vicky gave him a small smile. "I was just getting ready to leave." She stood up and started to gather her things. "I'll leave you to visit your brother."

Vicky said goodbye to Justin and Lee, walking out the room on shaking legs.

"Well?" Justin looked at Lee with raised eyebrows.

"Well, what?" Lee frowned at Justin. "Weren't you the one who sat here next to my bed telling me how seeing Georgia again was such a shock? But when you walked away, you realized that you had moved on from Georgia years ago. How she'd always be in your heart, but Vicky was more than just a part of your heart; she was a part of your soul?"

"I thought you were sleeping when I told you that?" Lee's eyes narrowed suspiciously.

"Yeah, I was desperately trying to," Justin said. "I really didn't want to have that awkward conversation with you."

"Thank you, brother!" Lee said, shaking his head. "I'm so glad you've always got my back and a sympathetic ear."

"No problem." Justin grinned. "So, stop standing there like a big idiot and go after her!"

"Now?" Lee said stupidly. He knew Justin was right.

"No," Justin shook his head. "Let's have some dinner first!" He picked up his pillow and threw it at Lee, who caught it. "Yes, now!"

"But she's gone...." Lee knew he was stalling. His heart was beating in his chest, and his mind was screaming at him to do what Justin said, but his feet were rooted to the spot.

"Oh, for goodness' sake!" Justin threw his blankets back and started to get out of bed.

"What are you doing?" Lee looked alarmed and moved towards his brother.

"Going to do what you're clearly too cowardly to do," Justin looked up at him. "I'm going to tell Vicky how you feel about her."

"No!" Lee helped Justin back into bed and put his pillow back into place. "I'll go."

"Good, then both of you go get me a burger," Justin ordered. "This food really sucks."

Lee shook his head at Justin before turning and running from the room.

Lee nearly bowled a few nurses and doctors over as he rushed out of the hospital, but he'd apologize later. His heart was racing in his chest at the exertion of the run and the prospect of telling Vicky she was wrong. That seeing Georgia, or Dawn as she now called herself, again hadn't changed how he felt about Vicky or the fact that she was the one he wanted to spend the rest of his life with.

Lee ran out of the hospital. His eyes scanned the area to see if he could find Vicky, and he did. She was buying an ice cream at the stand next to the hospital. Lee smiled and started to walk towards her. Vicky turned with a three scoop ice cream in her hand. Lee knew those scoops would be choc-mint, banana, and peanut butter. Vicky was about to take a lick of her ice cream when she saw him. She stopped and stared at him as he drew closer to her.

Lee stopped in front of Vicky and smiled down at her.

"Hi," Vicky said softly. Her beautiful eyes looked inquiringly up at him.

"You were wrong," Lee said to her. "Seeing Georgia again didn't change the way I feel about you. All it did was make me see you're the only want I want to spend the rest of my life with." He smiled as her beautiful eyes widened. "I love you and only you, Vicky."

"I love you too," Vicky breathed.

Lee pulled her to him, and their lips met, and once again, the world around them melted away. It wasn't until something cold hit Lee on the back of his neck that he realized they were standing blocking the sidewalk, and Vicky's ice cream was dripping down his neck.

"I think your ice cream's melting." Lee laughed, taking the

napkin she handed him and wiping his neck. "We'd better get Justin a burger, and we've been ordered back to his room."

"He's always been such a bossy boots," Vicky sighed. "Lazy but very, very bossy."

Lee took Vicky's hand as they walked towards the hamburger stand together. They had a lot of work ahead of them and they may still be in danger, but Lee had no doubt in his heart that together and with the help of his brother and sisters, they would sort this mystery out.

THE SERIES CONTINUES

ARE YOU READY TO READ Starting Over in Key West: You Can't Run Away Forever, book 3 of the Florida Keys Romance Series?

Go to https://www.amazon.com/dp/Bo9PTS23YV to read the next book in this series!

ALSO BY AMY RAFFERTY

THE SEA BREEZE COTTAGE - LA JOLLA COVE SERIES

Join Jennifer, her family, and friends as they learn that even the closest of families have secrets. Get tangled in the many twists and turns Jennifer, along with her family, starts to unravel as they dig up buried family pasts to reveal shocking revelations.

Go to https://www.amazon.com/dp/B08SK5TMGV to read the series

To get your FREE copy of the prequel to The Sea Breeze Cottage go to https://dl.bookfunnel.com/et26h8ozl3

Fallon and Piper McCaid have not spoken to each other in fifteen years, much to the despair of their younger sister, Ashley. With their brother missing, their grandfather in recovery, and their family home under threat, the sisters are reunited. The McCaid sisters are forced to put aside their differences to face their fears, unravel a mystery, and confront an unknown enemy.

Go to https://www.amazon.com/dp/B08YWP6RQB to read the series.

A MYSTERY AT SUMMER LODGE - A COASTAL VINEYARD SERIES

As Danielle and Nicole Cartwright take on each other's identities they soon come to realize life is not as cushy as they thought it was on the other side.

Go to https://www.amazon.com/dp/B094D7ZMJN to read the series.

To get your FREE copy of the prequel to A Mystery at Summer Lodge go to https://dl.bookfunnel.com/568ju6bskx

Join Erin and her family, Zane and his family, cousins Michael and Lilly as they scramble to sort out their lives, while all getting pulled into an adventure of a lifetime. A treasure hunt and mysterious secret beach caves that gets them all trapped in a potentially deadly situation. As they band together to face the dangers ahead, each one learns they may also be in danger of losing their hearts.

Go to https://www.amazon.com/dp/B093Z8WSPV to read the series.

CODY BAY INN - A NANTUCKET ROMANCE SERIES

The night was dark, wet, and electrified by the storm that ripped through the sky. Storms were not uncommon around Cody Bay but this storm was one Cody Moore would never forget.

Go to https://www.amazon.com/dp/B095MG7MZC to read the series.

To get your FREE copy of 'Nantucket Calling', the prequel to Cody Bay Inn go to https://dl.bookfunnel.com/eozhr4zdxk

STARTING OVER IN KEY WEST - A FLORIDA KEYS ROMANCE SERIES

Christy wasn't one for surprises, especially when they turned out to be the return of a man, she'd hoped never to set eyes on again— Aaron Butler. Unfortunately, it was inevitable their paths would collide when one of Christy's new recruits at the fire station was Aaron's son. And Aaron was not happy with his son's choice of career!

Go to https://www.amazon.com/dp/B09N2ZF4NV to read the series.

To get your FREE copy of 'Darkest Days, the prequel to Starting Over in Key West go to https://dl.bookfunnel.com/qjvtcnmcq5

Amy Rafferty

AUTHOR

STAY UPDATED WITH ME

Thank you so much for purchasing or downloading my book! I am grateful to all my amazing readers.

To stay updated on all my latest books, newsletters, freebies and beautiful photos from the fabulous locations I write about, why not join my VIP group?

I will send you regular pictures of La Jolla Cove, San Diego and the Florida Gulf Beaches where I try to spend as much time as I can. I live in San Diego, my own 'Garden Of Eden' and I am in love with the sea and the beaches in the area. They inspire me to write lots of beachy mystery romance fiction to share with my awesome readers like you. To join me go to https://landing.mailerlite.com/webforms/landing/y6w2d2

You will be asked for your email. You also get a FREE BOOK whenever you sign-up!

FREE BOOK

To get your free copy of the prequel to the Amazon #1 Best-Seller 'Starting Over in Key West' go to https://dl.bookfunnel.com/qjvtcnmcq5

ABOUT THE AUTHOR

Amazon #1 Best-Seller, Amy Rafferty is a contemporary romance author of feel-good beach romance reads with heartwarming stories embracing humor and love.

Born in New York, previously a Lawyer, she now lives in San Diego with her beautiful children and cats!

Aside from writing, publishing and running her home, she spends as much time as she can visiting the beautiful San Diego and Florida beaches where she has family and friends. She calls San Diego her 'Garden of Eden', inspiring her to write clean and wholesome romance novels incorporating mystery, suspense and adventures for her characters as they find a way to open their hearts and let true love in.

facebook.com/amyraffertyauthor

instagram.com/amyraffertyauthor